HAUNTED GRAVE

MADAME CHALAMET GHOST MYSTERIES 5

BYRD NASH

ROOK AND CASTLE PRESS
SAINT CHARLES, ILLINOIS

CONTENTS

Books by Byrd Nash   vi

Chapter 1   1
Chapter 2   13
Chapter 3   21
Chapter 4   29
Chapter 5   37
Chapter 6   45
Chapter 7   53
Chapter 8   59
Chapter 9   67
Chapter 10   75
Chapter 11   83
Chapter 12   93
Chapter 13   101
Chapter 14   111
Chapter 15   119
Chapter 16   127
Chapter 17   133
Chapter 18   141
Chapter 19   151
Chapter 20   157
Chapter 21   167
Chapter 22   175
Chapter 23   183
Chapter 24   193
Epilogue   197

Author Notes   199
Cast of Characters   201

Books by Byrd Nash

Madame Chalamet Ghost Mysteries

Ghost Talker #1

Delicious Death #2

Spirit Guide #3

Gray Lady #4

Haunted Grave #5

Ghastly Mistake #6

Contemporary, Magical Realism

A Spell of Rowans

College Fae Series

Never Date a Siren #1

A Study in Spirits #2

Bane of Hounds #3

Romantic Fairytales

Dance of Hearts (Cinderella retelling)

Price of a Rose (Beauty and the Beast retelling)

Fairytale Fantasy

The Wicked Wolves of Windsor and other Fairytales

*"The grave itself is but a covered bridge,
Leading from light to light, through a brief darkness!"*
Henry Wadsworth Longfellow

Dedications
To my readers,
who waited

CHAPTER ONE

S aving a king's life wasn't worth much.

Returning to Alenbonné, fresh from my adventure with the Gray Lady, I visited the university seeking my dear friend, Charlotte LaRue. To my surprise, the school was mostly empty despite it being early fall when the next semester should be in session. A note on her office door stated I could find her at home.

She had a set of rooms in a three-story flat, and it would have been easy to mistake the place as that of a student because of the mismatched furniture, worn seat cushions, and stained carpet. However, it was only a sign of Charlotte's careless negligence to everything that wasn't her work.

I opened the door after a yelled, "enter!"

Sprawled on the sofa, Charlotte was reading the newspaper. Despite it being the early afternoon, she still wore a velvet dressing gown over her trousers and shirt. Her feet were bare. She sat up, exclaiming over the back of her couch, "Elinor! When did you get back?"

"About an hour ago. I came straight here because of an urgent matter. By chance, you haven't recently received a letter from me, have you?"

Tossing the newspaper aside, she rose to her feet and, from a cubbyhole of her desk, pulled out a slim pack of folded papers. "Is this the one you mean?"

"Yes, thank you."

"As you wrote in your letter, I didn't read them. Anything I need to know about?" She handed them to me with open curiosity, but I wasn't going to discuss the king's private papers or how we almost got arrested because the king's man, de Windt, thought Tristan had stolen them. It was bad enough that his sister Valentina was involved because of Lady Josephine blackmailing her.

Placing the packet in my purse, I replied, "Probably the less you know, the better. As it is, I almost got arrested because of these things."

She chuckled. "Sounds like a story I'll want to hear. When you can tell it."

Looking around the room, I noticed that books littered the floor and there was a tray of day-old food on a nearby chair. "By the way, why are you here in the middle of the week, instead of in your offices?"

She shrugged. "Classes are out this week due to the protests."

Students were always upset about something or another. With my thoughts on my problems, I paid her information little heed. "By the way, did you speak to His Grace about me? Telling him I needed a holiday?"

Charlotte responded promptly. "I did. You weren't taking me seriously enough after that business with Lafayette, but I figured he'd get you to do it. And here you are, returned to our city of fog and rain with a bloom in your cheeks and a little weight on you."

Suddenly overcome, I took her in a crushing hug. "Thank you, dear friend. I had a wonderful time."

Releasing her, I told her, "Now I need to run. We will catch up later."

As I was trotting down the stairs, she leaned over the balcony landing, telling me, "Look, be careful out there today, will you?"

I waved up at her. "Of course I will!"

"There's no 'of course' about it." The seriousness of her tone halted me. I looked up at her. "I'm always careful."

She rolled her eyes dramatically. "You are in no way careful. Things are a bit rocky out there, so just be aware of where you are and who is around you, all right? Now, look, since you are back in town, I have someone who needs your assistance. Can I bring him by the Crown tomorrow? For tea?"

"Certainly!"

Outside, I climbed back into the quick-cab I had told to wait at the curb for me, and rapped smartly on the roof. "The residency, please."

Our journey was not as fast as I would have liked. We ran into blocked streets, and gendarmes stopped us and asked the driver to show his license. After we pulled away from the second inquisition about who we were and what our business was, I opened the roof hatch and called up to my driver, "What is this all about?"

"You must have been away, madame. Them students been causing a ruckus, and the government wants them shut down. Roads to the residency are all being watched by the gendarmes."

I closed the hatch and reclined back on the seat. This seemed excessive for student protests. When I had time to talk with Charlotte tomorrow, I would ask her for more details.

The residency included a group of buildings which held the staff of the Sarnesse government. The palace was centrally located in the complex, and it was the home for King Guénard whenever he was in town. Next to it, and built later and with far less panache, were two squat utilitarian buildings. Beside the more elegant palace, they squatted like bull dogs next to a swan.

We were once again stopped, this time by traffic. We were still several blocks away, but I could see the central dome of the palace over the rooftops. After waiting for ten minutes with no movement, I opened the hatch again and paid the driver. "I'll get out here. It will be quicker if I just walk."

"You sure, madame? Looks to be some sort of protest going on ahead. Might be best to call another day."

No. Those letters were burning a hole in my purse and I wanted them out of my hands. I reassured him. "I'll be fine."

Unfortunately, the driver's opinion proved right. Gendarme blocked the thoroughfare as they pressed back a crowd of protesters, who seemed to be a mixed group of women and men of the working class. They carried signs demanding lower taxes and protections for factory workers. Hardly students.

It would have taken me longer to shove my way through them, but Inspector Marcellus Barbier, my old friend among the gendarmes, spotted me. A small, tidy man dressed in the everyday working man's brown tweed and bowler hat, Barbier limped over to me.

"Let her through!" he barked to his men, and they shoved the crowd back, making a way for me through the barricade.

"What are you doing here, Elinor? Here to see His Grace, by chance?"

I felt the heat rise to my cheeks at his question. Busying myself by tucking up a lock of hair that had fallen free from its pin, I asked nonchalantly, "Oh? Is the Duke de Archambeau here?"

"Just saw his carriage go around the back way to the private entrance. Safer to enter the Residence through the tunnel for now."

"Well, perhaps I'll see him another time. I'm here to drop off a legal filing, that is all."

The inspector looked past me, his gaze upon the crowd. The long furrows on either side of his mouth deepened, giving him a gaunt look. He seemed worn down, but filled with energy at the same time. "Hurry and do it. This crowd is getting restless and things could get messy here. It's no place for a girl like yourself."

"Why such fervor now, inspector?"

He grunted, shoving his hands in his pockets. Rocking back and forth on the balls of his feet to his heels, his shorter leg gave him a pitched tilt.

"Huge factory lay-off down at the bottling plant. Some fella made an invention that does the work of twenty. It's put them out of work, so they have plenty of time to come over here and moan about their empty bellies."

"You don't seem to have much sympathy for them? As a working man yourself, that surprises me."

He shrugged. "A man makes his own way in this world. If you have the drive, you shape your future."

If you were trained to do one job, how hard would it be to find another? But Barbier could be stubborn and I didn't want to argue. "By the way, where is Sergeant Dupont? I thought you'd need him here to manage this crowd."

"Gone," Barbier growled. "Took off right after the Lafayette case. So here I am, a man short, no thanks to him."

"How strange. Why did he do that?"

"No idea. He hasn't come by to get the last pay he's owed, and he's no longer at his lodgings. If I could find him, I'd box his ears."

My suspicions about Dupont having had something to do with Parnell's death grew. He was the only one present when Parnell jumped from the staircase to his death. Or so he said that was what happened.

It did not fit that the arrogant man would have done such a thing and Parnell's death produced a dead end. Who had he worked with to develop his horrible drug? Who knew, and how, to take Parnell's research before we could retrieve it?

"Does his family know where he is gone?"

"No family. His parents died long ago, and his half-sister passed about a year ago. What's your interest in him?"

"Oh, I was just curious." Before he could ask anything else, there was a shout from one of his men which made Barbier mutter, "These idiots. I've got to go. Elinor, get your business

done and get back to the Crown. This is no place today for a
lady."

I fully intended on taking the inspector's advice, but trying to see
King Guénard without an appointment proved difficult.

"Is this something that one of us can handle, madame?" asked
the clerk at the front desk where I had been told to make my
inquiries.

"No. I must speak to him directly. I promise it will only take a
moment." There was no way I was handing these letters off to
someone I didn't know. What would be the point of secretly
bringing them all this way, only to see them fall into the wrong
hands all over again?

"Sign in here." He handed me a pen and a registry where
others before me had made their requests. Judging from the long
list and those who were still waiting in the hall, I was at the end of
a queue that didn't look to be moving quickly.

After signing my name, the clerk pointed to where I should
wait and I took my seat in a hardbacked chair. As time passed, I
occupied my mind by guessing how long each person's problem
would take and what they wanted. A few went through the doors
and were immediately tossed back, like a catch that wasn't big
enough. Inevitably, their faces showed various degrees of anger,
frustration, or despair. Were they wanting money? A position?
Relief for a loved one?

Most, though, had longer audiences and the afternoon
dragged on as my stomach growled, a reminder that I had
skipped lunch. I bent my neck to either side to work the kinks
out of it.

Around three in the afternoon, a man dressed in black and
carrying a leather bag stopped in front of me. When he called my
name, I shook off my ennui. It took me a moment to recognize

him; he was King Guénard's royal physician, whom I had met briefly at Lindengaard during the Winter Revels.

"Dr. Hagen." I was about to stand, but he waved for me to keep my seat and took the empty one next to mine.

"How are you and your friend, Dr. LaRue?"

"We are both fine, doctor. Thank you for asking." I did not ask about His Majesty, for what could he say in this public place but that the king was well?

In a low voice so as not to be overheard, he told me, "Excellent work, she did, though at the time I may not have expressed my appreciation for her efforts." He readjusted the glasses on his nose, peering at me through their thick lenses. "Are you here to meet His Majesty?"

"I had hoped to, but I did not have an appointment, and it seems there are others with the same thought."

He had very dark brown eyes, magnified by the lenses, and they examined me intently. "Is it urgent? For I seem to recall that most things involving you are?"

I couldn't help but smile. "I do wish to see him today. It will not take long, but it is a private matter I cannot discuss with anyone but His Majesty, I'm afraid. I promise it will greatly interest him."

He stood up and gestured for me to follow him. "I am about to conduct my daily wellness check. You shall serve as my nurse."

No one stopped the doctor, and the clerk at the desk only gave him a bow of respect as we passed by. He opened a smaller door next to the grand double door entrance where other claimants had entered. This led to a side room connected to the primary receiving room. It was very grand, with dark paneled walls, rich velvet drapes on the one window looking out over the square, and antique furniture.

The doctor set his bag on a small round side table and started pulling out his medical equipment. "His Majesty will be here shortly. My visit gives him a break from dealing with requests and a chance for me to make sure his blood pressure hasn't climbed too high."

"I hope His Majesty is doing better since his time at Lindengaard?"

"He survived it," was all the doctor would share.

The door opened, and the egg-shaped form of King Guénard entered. He was complaining bitterly to the person behind him. "If you bring me one more who wants to complain about the drains, I shall send you off to Zulskaya where you can freeze your private regions bare-assed on a mountain!"

Trying to balance a tall stack of papers in her hands, the clerk said, "I'm sorry, Your Majesty. However, if they request a hearing from you, I must allow them a chance to plead their case. It is, after all, the law."

King Guénard waved his clerk away with a fluttering hand. "The law! Hang the law! Go get my tea and don't dally! I'll barely have time to gulp it down if I'm to see all this lot before the end of the day."

The door closed, and his attention swung my direction. I sank into a deep curtsy.

"Madame Chalamet. Hm. Well, I hope you aren't here to tell me another one of my nobles is intending to murder me?"

"No, Your Majesty." At first, Guénard seemed unchanged. Yet, as I examined him closely, the gray in his dark brown hair had increased and the wrinkles around his eyes and on his forehead were deeper since we had last met. His face had a pasty cast to it, and a coating of make-up only made it look worse.

I took a deep breath and said, "I am here to bring back some personal papers that you might be missing." Reaching into my bag, I handed them over to him. He broke my wax seal and glanced through them quickly.

"A-ha! So you were involved just like I thought!" After a moment more, he said, "All here. Good. Now sit. I cannot have my afternoon tea until Dr. Hagen makes sure if my heart can take it."

I perched myself on the edge of a chair, ready to take flight. I could feel cold sweat in my armpits and I tucked my fingers under a fold of my dress to hide the tension they held. King Guénard looked like a fool, and perhaps he behaved like one, but he was still our king. And his mood was famous for being unpredictable.

Dr. Hagen had said nothing during our exchange and was listening to the king's heart with his stethoscope. Repositioning it, he said, "Take a deep breath."

During this examination, the clerk returned with a servant pushing a tea cart. The finger bread, cheese, figs, and olives with tea and coffee, as well as an unopened bottle of Chambaux wine, made my stomach ache. But no one invited me to partake, so I tried my best to ignore the bounty before me.

"All of you out, except for Madame Chalamet and Dr. Hagen." With bows his servants and staff scurried away. Once the door closed behind them, King Guénard demanded, "My letters, madame, how did you come by them? From Tristan Fontaine by chance?"

"No, Your Majesty. They came to me via Lady Josephine Baudelaire who had hoped to use them to harm the Duke de Archambeau by incriminating him in a theft he had no hand in."

His face held a moment of surprise before showing speculation. "Lady Baudelaire? Oh yes, I remember, she's a confidante to one of my latest paramours. How would she get these? They were inside my personal desk in my rooms."

"I do not know, Your Majesty." Josephine Baudelaire had obviously had her friend take them, but it would be best not to voice my suspicions and let him figure it out. Least said, soonest mended.

He may have read my mind, or at least my expression. "Nothing else to say, Madame Chalamet? As I recall, you like to talk." He tapped the folded letters against his forehead as he continued to survey me. "Sven de Windt reported to me this morning about events at Hightower. Strange doings there."

"Yes, Your Majesty."

"Yes— no— yes," he parroted back at me. "You might as well be a stage puppet. I do not remember you being so reticent before in your speech."

I regretted not confiding the problem to Tristan and letting him return the letters, but I had promised Valentina to keep him out of it. King Guénard could be tetchy and I had little experience in understanding his moods or how to handle him. His capricious use of power to punish those who displeased him was legendary.

I needed to move the conversation away from the letters to the murder of Lord Montaine while remembering my promise to Lady Montaine. I said, "I believe her husband's doctor misled Lady Odette Tremblay into giving him a potion of hallucinogenic drugs that resulted in his death. And possibly madness. However, I do not think Lady Tremblay understood the full ramifications of what she was being advised to do."

"So, in your estimation, she is to be held blameless for her husband's condition?" His tone was detached, but his gaze was piercing.

Staying as calm as I could, I replied, "If, in his madness, brought on by drugs, Lord Tremblay murdered Lord Montaine, how can I blame his wife? She was told to give her husband that drink by a medical man. Would any woman wishing her husband well refuse a doctor's advice?"

"Ha. Doctors always think they know best, don't they, Hagen?"

Dr. Hagen murmured, "And we are usually right, Your Majesty."

I said nothing more and finally, the king gave judgment. "Well, you can put your mind at ease. It's unlikely the law would prosecute a woman of the nobility for such a crime. There are legal protections that her bloodline and gender provide. It would be a terrible precedent to see a lady in court defending her life on such a grubby charge. Besides Tremblay is dead. Very tidy."

There was a tap on the door and which made the king give another aggravated, "Come in!" His clerk returned with her stack of papers, reminding him, "Your Majesty, if we are to stay on schedule—"

"Close that door," he ordered her. Opening a bottle, he poured himself a glass, before reaching for a petit fours.

"No," said Dr. Hagen firmly. "We agreed to moderation. The wine or the sweet. Not both."

Giving his doctor an aggrieved look, the king did as his physician ordered. It went down in two gulps. Wiping his hands with a napkin, he asked me casually, "No reward for these letters, madame? You are singularly quiet about compensation."

I gave a faint smile. "There is only one thing I want and that you cannot give me."

Before he could ask, there was a tap on the door. At his "Come!" Tristan Fontaine, the Duke de Archambeau entered. *How inconvenient!*

CHAPTER TWO

Seeing me, Tristan's face froze and then wiped itself clean of any expression. It had been a week since I had seen him, yet I felt an overwhelming need to rush into his arms even if he was standing there as friendly as an icicle.

He sketched a bow to the king. His northern accent a bit more pronounced than usual, the only sign of his perturbation as he spoke, "As you requested, I am here."

"Never mind. The intrepid Madame Chalamet resolved my problem," said King Guénard dismissively. He held up the letters high over his head in triumph before pointing them towards me.

"How fortunate for you, your majesty," was Tristan's cool response, his eyes opaque. It had been a long time since I had been on the receiving end of Tristan's coldness and I found I didn't like it. It made me want to give him a good shake.

"It seems Lady Josephine Baudelaire is not a friend of yours. Madame Chalamet says accusing you of the theft of these letters was a plot by her to discredit you."

"Women seldom are my friends," Tristan replied stiffly.

"She returned them and now says she doesn't want a reward.

Says I can't give her what she wants. Do you believe that? I think she's holding out for something more and taking advantage of my good nature."

It took a keen observer to know that under his chilly exterior, Tristan was about to burst into flame. The snowy mountain concealed a volcano. The corners of his lips had tightened slightly, and the faint crow lines at his eyes had deepened due to an almost imperceptible narrowing of his eyes.

King Guénard was not the man to notice such, and continued, his attention shifting to someone else. "I want this Baudelaire woman investigated."

"It's already underway, Your Majesty. We found a jewel of hers in a criminal's stolen hoard tying her to an illegal transaction. We believe she is involved with those undermining Your Majesty's reign. This theft of your letters would be part of that."

"Yes. Yes," the king muttered. "But what have you done about it?"

"She's under surveillance. We need more evidence before making a move against a lady so well connected."

King Guénard was not a patient man. "You keep talking about investigations, but have you seen what's outside today? A mob of idiots! Protesting that they have to work for their bread! You need to take care of them. Haul them off! Throw them in prison."

"That isn't my department. That's de Windt's domain. The man you sent to arrest me."

"Are you holding that against me? I had to do something! Rumors were flying, and the courtiers were calling for your head. Especially after that thing with your wife. They've never trusted you again. You can't blame me for that."

There was another knock on the door that adjoined the receiving room. Guénard snapped, "What now?"

The clerk from earlier opened the door and poked only her head inside. "We are falling behind schedule, Your Majesty."

"Yes, I love meeting more people who demand impossible things from me!" he muttered under his breath. Dr. Hagen's check-up completed, he roughly pulled down his sleeve and, after fastening the cuff, put on his coat, all while issuing orders to Tristan. "Deal with that Baudelaire woman. I don't care if she is the friend of my latest." He added menacingly, "If you can't do it with the courts, remove her another way that sends a message. No one steals my personal correspondence. No one."

He exited. Before I could say anything, Tristan turned on his heel and also left, choosing the door I had entered. "Thank you, Dr. Hagen, for your assistance," I hurriedly told the king's personal physician before rushing out the door after him.

Tristan was storming down the hall, back stiff, his hands balled at his side. Rushing after him caused curious glances to be cast our way, but I ignored them. I needed to talk with him or risk more damage from what had happened in there.

When I reached his side, seeing his stony profile, I told him quietly, "It is not what he implied. His Majesty exaggerated things."

He stared straight ahead. "Why did you not tell me about those letters when we were at Hightower?"

"Please!" I begged, noticing more stares coming our way. "Is there somewhere private we can talk?"

There was, but it took a while to get to his office. With one glance at Tristan's face, his secretary, Stephan, fled the room. Tristan closed the door behind him very carefully, very softly.

"Your explanation, madame?" Being in love with him demanded a stout constitution, so his icy voice did not daunt me. This was not how I had planned on telling Tristan about his sister being blackmailed by Josephine, but circumstances were forcing my hand.

"I discovered the letters when I was at Hightower. Before de Windt arrived. To keep them safe, I posted them to Charlotte.

When I returned to Alenbonné, I felt getting them back to His Majesty as quickly as possible without involving you was the best thing to do. That way, de Windt couldn't accuse you of knowing anything about them."

"Without involving me?!" he exploded. "It's my neck on the chopping block so I think I'm very much involved, madame!"

"Please, Tristan. I wanted to tell you everything, but not like this."

"In what way were you going to tell me? You are being forced to explain, because I caught you going behind my back. I should have known you were as duplicitous as all of your sex."

"Do not lump me with others, and especially not with *her*. I have done nothing against you, ever." My temper was rising, as were our voices. "I am not going to defend my actions when you are in this foul mood."

"Leave then." He leaned against his desk, half sitting on it, arms folded, his expression remote as he turned his face away from me. This stony reply made me waver. Should I let him stew or fight it out? If I did not try, would a man as proud as him come to me?

Taking a deep breath, I tried again. "I did intend to tell you about the letters, but de Windt arrived accusing you of treason! It didn't seem the right time to let you know about them when he thought you had stolen them in the first place!"

"How did you find those letters? Where?" he demanded.

There was no way around it. I would have to tell him about Valentina and her involvement in Josephine's plot to discredit him. "Your sister gave them to me." He blinked, showing the first sign of surprise, but still he did not soften. His mouth only became thinner at the mention of Valentina.

"Please," I begged him, tentatively touching his crossed arms with my fingertips. "Will you really listen and let me tell you what happened?"

"Go ahead." He sank his chin to his chest and closed his eyes, like a man bracing for a blow. A blow that would come from someone he cared for, from people he loved.

"Our man, our master criminal, needs to remove you. You're the king's man and with you gone, or deemed untrustworthy, Guénard would have less competent people around him— people like de Windt."

"So you also think it was a plot?"

"Valentina told me that Josephine was in deep with moneylenders, hence why she was trying to pressure you into marriage. When you did not take the bait, she rushed off to marry, and used that stone from her husband's family necklace to pay off who she owed. But, I don't think it was enough. Or perhaps she tried to pay it off, but they refused? It would explain why the stone was sitting in a safe and not sold off. It was being held until she did something for them." I shook my head. "This is only a guess, but I think she was told to get someone close to you in a compromising situation so they would have a way to get at you."

"You mean my sister?"

"I doubt they would have been brave enough to approach your mother," I pointed out. That comment at least elicited a grunt; it wasn't a sneer but still less than a chuckle. I pressed onward. "Valentina viewed her as a friend, and because she had her guard down, Josephine seduced her into doing a harmful prank."

It only took him a moment to guess. "The fall down the stairs?"

I nodded. "I don't think your sister meant for Lady Annabel van den Berg to get seriously hurt. But when she did, Josephine made sure society remembered the incident."

"Ah. I think I'm beginning to see. The gossip I blamed Val for spreading was really Josephine?"

"Yes. Repeating the story at soirées was a way to remind Valentina of what Josephine could reveal. At Hightower, Josephine gave Valentina the letters and told her to plant them in your belongings. Or else she would reveal her complicity in the prank that broke Lady van den Berg's arm. Instead, she hid them in Lord Montaine's library for safekeeping. If she had had time, I feel sure she would have told you this herself, but de Windt showed up and started threatening you."

While I had confessed to Valentina's involvement, I was not going to speak of what had happened at the beach picnic on the cliff side. That was his sister's to share, or not.

Tristan gave a heavy sigh. "Yes, it was a set-up by someone here at the Residency. Guénard heard a story from his mistress that I was compromised and he had to send de Windt to investigate. He could have done no less. She was telling everyone that I was a traitor, and because of Minette's machinations so long ago that slandered my name, it was being readily believed."

He said the last with a weary air; it didn't look like he had slept much since leaving Hightower. I came closer, placing my hand now on his upper arm. "How tired you look."

Slowly, almost hesitantly, his arm slipped around my waist and he brought me against him, his forehead resting against the top line of my shoulder. His voice sounded sad and exhausted. "Never do this to me again, Elinor. I thought— I thought you had betrayed me. I do not think I could survive that."

My hand came up around the back of his head, my fingers tangling in his hair, as I kissed his temple. "I would never betray you. Give you a heart attack from shock, or lie about what I'm doing for a good cause, perhaps, but I'd never betray you."

He gave a watery chuckle and squeezed me before meeting my eyes. "You are going to be nothing but trouble, aren't you?"

"I think you like trouble."

"When it comes from you, yes, but from the king?" He shook his head. "I'm getting too old for this game. My heart seized up when I saw you in there with him, wondering if he had summoned you as a pawn in one of his political games. Or worse, that you had played me. He implied as much."

"He was trying to get a rise from you. I think I'll confine

myself to ghosts in the future. They are much easier to deal with than kings. Am I forgiven?"

"I must. I have no other option."

"You don't have to say it like you are mounting the steps to the gallows! You could choose to keep me at a distance, punishing me by disappearing for months on end. Forcing me to run you down with the Ladies Safety Edition bicycle to get your attention."

That gained me a smile. "I have a present for you."

"Some expensive bauble to appease me?" I asked, eyebrows raised.

"I'll let you decide." He released me and, going around his desk, pulled open a drawer to retrieve a roll of soft black leather. Curious, I pulled the string that tied it closed and unrolled it so it lay flat on the desk.

"Oh, Tristan!" I lovingly pulled out the brass lock-picking tools from their pockets and held them up to my eye to admire them.

"I saw that you admired my set and thought you'd like your own."

"Are they very hard to use?"

"Not really. It's more about patience and experimenting with different locks."

"Perhaps you can come over and instruct me?"

"It sounds far more entertaining than what I need to take care of today. Unfortunately, I can't. Things are in a dangerous flux around here. Petty squabbles, ready to become vendettas. But tomorrow? Before this horrible muddle, I planned to invite you to the theater tomorrow evening. Will you be free?"

"Yes."

His hand came up to stroke my cheek before he gave me a deep, intense kiss. I could see there was something to be said about making up after a fight.

Finally, he broke away. "Now, get out of here." He pushed me gently towards the door. "I have at least three meetings, and witnesses to interrogate, before I can leave here."

Opening the door, I paused and asked, "What shall I wear?"

"I'm sure you know what I'd like."

I laughed. Passing Stephan in the outer office, I informed Tristan's secretary, "I've put your boss into a much nicer temper. Be sure to take care of him for me."

CHAPTER THREE

Back at the Crown, I was halfway through my stack of correspondence when Anne-Marie interrupted me, newspaper in hand. "Lady Annabel van den Berg is having a party tonight."

I turned halfway in my seat. "Interesting. What type of party?"

She read aloud, "To celebrate her birthday."

"Hm. Good work, Anne-Marie." I had told her to keep an eye out for any information about the woman injured by the trip-wire installed by Josephine and Valentina. Here was a chance to end Josephine's blackmail scheme once and for all. "Be sure to have my black dress, the dramatic one, and the veil ready for tonight. I will be paying Lady van den Berg a visit."

She was in the bedroom finding my dress when there was a tap on the door. I answered it to find Charlotte and the man she wanted me to meet, Dr. Armand Devereaux.

"Please, take a seat," I gestured to a chair opposite. Charlotte took another chair, sitting next to Dr. Devereaux.

Devereaux was on the short side for a man, with shoulders barely wider than his waist, and wiry black hair that was going prematurely gray. His large dark eyes held a gravity to them that made you wonder if he had a secret sorrow, and the man's voice was rich and deep, in fact, gorgeous, to listen to.

"Dr. Devereaux is one of the attending physicians at the Bellwether House," Charlotte explained. Bellwether was a charity hospital which dealt with a variety of health problems of the poor. "He has a patient that I think you can help him with."

"I don't use my medical training in the way you might expect, Madame Chalamet. I do not set bones or stitch broken heads. I mend hearts and fix the mind. It is why I can practice medicine despite this." With his left hand, the doctor lifted his right hand, which was half the length of his regular arm. The difference did not seem to be from an accident as the arm was naturally formed and the appendage moved as well as the other. "Instead, I use my mind and help those who have lost their way. People who can no longer function fully within our society. Those classed as lunatics, who have dementia or melancholia. These are my patients."

"Please go on," I said. "I am fascinated by this new field that has emerged with the talk therapy. That is what you do, is it not?"

"Yes. However, while I do have weekly rounds at Bellwether, I also maintain a private practice. That is what I wish to speak with you about." He spared a glance towards Charlotte, who gave him an encouraging nod as she lit her cigaretto and said, "You can trust her. Anything you say will remain confidential."

This was the story he related:

A few months back, I saw a patient at my home office who was new to my practice. Though he had made an appointment with my clerk, at the time he had refused to explain what the problem was he wanted to consult with me about.

This is a relatively common fear for my patients. The idea of seeking help for any disorder of the mind is still viewed with vast suspicion and distrust. It is a thing I hope to see changed with my work. So his reticence did not surprise me at that time, though later—

When I met Mysir Forrest Boutin, he struck me as typical of the merchant class. In his mid-sixties, he had a well-fed, fleshy physique with high blood pressure and the beginning of cataracts. Otherwise, he seemed in good health with nothing physically out of the ordinary with him.

Yet, he was a nervous man. He made his appointment for the end of the day when my waiting room was normally empty, and kept checking the hall, as if worried someone would be lurking there.

My office is on the second floor and no passerby would hear anything said in that room. However, I did as he requested. Dealing with what seems to be unreasonable requests is part of what I deal with on a daily basis. I thought perhaps his suspicious nature was part of his malady.

It took time for him to come to the point. This is also not unusual. It takes careful questioning and patience to have patients reveal their innermost fears. I am told that I project a calm and confiding nature, so do tend to have success in this, and so eventually he told me about his fear of dying. Or, to be exact, a fear of being buried alive.

My profession has a name for this condition: taphephobia. I believe it to be related to the fear of enclosed places, and is a common enough concern that I see it often in my practice.

There is also a type of nightmare, called frozen sleeping, where a person becomes incapable of moving after they wake. It doesn't last long, but the idea of paralysis, combined with a fear of enclosed places, leads some to believe they are being buried alive.

There have been some poor medical practices that resulted in a few, very few, individuals who have lapsed into a coma to be buried by mistake. The popular press grossly exaggerates the occurrences.

However, Mysir Forrest Boutin's fear took an exceptional

form. He believed his enemies would make sure he experienced a 'living death.'

Yes, I see this amazes you as it did me! At first, I thought he had scheming relatives after his money. As we age, sometimes we get it into our heads that others in our family do not have our best interests at heart. But no. He had never married, and had no children. He had no business partners.

When I inquired who might hurt him in such a matter, he grew quite cagey. It is not surprising that patients are reluctant to divulge their beliefs, since they could be declared unfit and thus institutionalized. Unfortunately, I've seen this happen when such a sentence would financially benefit another.

It takes time to build confidence in a doctor-patient relationship, and thus it took several sessions to learn the full extent of his story. He was on the outs with some former business associates and felt they would want revenge upon him because of some imagined wrong. Mysir Boutin said he knew of others who had died conveniently.

His business? He is a wool merchant! Yet to hear him talk of them, you would think the men he plies his trade with are the most bloodthirsty pirates this side of Perino!

However, I often see these irrational beliefs in my practice, so I was not at first alarmed. That is until he showed me this at our last appointment.

He handed me a piece of torn paper with an inked symbol on it that made no sense to me. It was a circle with three slashes, two of them forming an x over the vertical central slash.

Mysir Boutin said it was the sign he feared for it was a message from his associates that death was near. He had quit his lodgings just that morning and begged me to hide him. If I provided him with aid and met some other humble conditions, he would leave me a legacy. A gift for my new ward at Bellwether for treating mind disorders of the less fortunate.

Of course I would be interested in that! I'd be a fool not to do so. However, would that be taking an unfair advantage of him and might cause to worsen his condition? Doctors, especially those who understand the human heart, need to keep a professional distance from patients. Our special knowledge allows us to easily manipulate them. I have seen some of my fellow doctors behave less scrupulously and it always ended in disaster.

However, the money would mean a great deal to so many. Thus, against my better judgment, I agreed that he could lodge in the apartment above my offices.

That floor of the house I reserve for patients who need extensive but private attention, such as those withdrawing from addictions to alcohol or drugs. Some patients, due to their standing in society, can afford such accommodations. I'm sure you can understand why families would prefer keeping their problems as private as possible. That is not always possible in a public ward or institution.

After he toured the rooms, which are very secure, with bars on the windows, we agreed to a brief stay until he could make other arrangements.

Now, let me tell you of my household staff, for they are also important in this tale. There is my clerk and a boy who answers the door for me. Both of them are only there during working hours. I have a cleaner and a cook, neither of them live in. I sometimes employ a Bellwether nurse for when the patient requires more attention than I can personally provide. All are trustworthy people who have been with me for over a decade, except for the boy, who is the younger brother of my clerk.

They are not strangers.

Last week, on Thursday, it was late in the afternoon when I was scheduled to meet a new patient, a Madame Michelle Mazet. With new patients, I usually do an intake session discussing their health and what treatment they need.

Madame Mazet arrived early, and the boy who let her in decided to take a trip down to the street corner to buy a newssheet.

He later told me this was at the lady's bidding and she had given him a coin to run this errand.

He was barely out the door when she collapsed into a dead faint. It took both my clerk and me to bring her into my examination room, where she could recover herself. This left my lobby, where the staircase to the upper floor is unattended. Something I realized only later was important, as you will understand when you hear the rest.

It seemed Madame Mazet was of the hysterical type for once she recovered enough to sit up and take a sip of sherry, she declared she could not meet with me. She said, the cause of her collapse was that upon entering the lobby she had seen an orange cat, and she was deathly afraid of cats.

I reassured her that the only cat in residence is a black one that Cook keeps in the kitchen and roams only the cellar. We had no orange cat. However, there is no arguing with people in that state. She had it in her head that she had seen a cat, and it was pointless to convince her otherwise. She soon left.

Before I closed my office for the day, Mysir Boutin burst through the door in a rage. He insisted someone had been in his room, examining his things. He first accused my staff. Then myself. We were all outraged at his accusations, and the household was in an uproar with Cook crying and my clerk threatening to quit.

Mysir Boutin was reticent on explaining exactly how he knew someone had invaded his personal suite upstairs or who they might be. But thinking about Madame Mazet's visit and my disappearing page boy, I believe someone may have entered the house while we were dealing with her faint.

Who that person was or their intention remains unclear to me.

The incident set back Mysir Boutin's state of mind. Now he spends most of his time in bed, stating that he will die soon. Two days ago, he summoned his lawyer and made a new will. They showed it to me.

I must fulfill certain duties, and if these are done, Bellwether shall receive over one million royals! I never thought the man had so much money! The amount of good it could do for my patients is vast, but I cannot help but feel guilty since this invasion of his privacy happened at my residence. It was due to my staff's negligence that he had entered such a depression!

A few days ago, I asked Dr. LaRue's advice on the matter. She suggested I consult with you. Death is your specialty, as the murdered are hers, and the mind is mine. So here I am, seeking your help, Madame Chalamet, for I do not even know where to begin.

Under the will's condition, I must first ensure that a medical doctor, other than myself, declares him dead. That his flesh will not animate again. Dr. LaRue agreed to help me with this condition.

Second, he is to be buried in a certain city cemetery. His coffin shall be without a lid for a fourteen-day vigil, and I must make sure there is a trustworthy guard on duty at all times. Even I must be on watch and spend the night there myself.

Once the vigil passes, the lid is to be fastened, and the grave filled. A month later, I am to return and have him disinterred in the presence of a police officer and his lawyer. If there is any evidence that he tried to escape his coffin after burial, I lose the money.

It's absurd! Ridiculous!

Yet I cannot help but feel that there is some real danger here. The man believes this will happen, though he appears to be a sane man. I am puzzled. Thus, I lay the matter before you.

CHAPTER FOUR

"How fascinating," I told Dr. Devereaux. "I would love to meet Mysir Boutin if you think he would be open to that."

"That is what I had hoped," he said eagerly. "When I discussed the problem with Dr. LaRue at our club, she mentioned you might provide a wider spiritual perspective to him. Help ease his fears about dying and what comes afterward."

"I have counseled the dying, but not in any medical way. I only provide my personal experiences that there is an Afterlife, an existence past our bodily one here on the earthly plane. If he would welcome my visit, I am more than ready to help."

Charlotte stood up. "Sorry, Elinor, but I'm needed down at the morgue and can't linger for a good chat."

I rose too and walked to the door with them, bidding them goodbye with an assurance from Dr. Devereaux that he would be in contact with me.

After my guests left, I decided to take a walk along the canal to clear my mind before dinner. It wasn't long before Jacques Moreau appeared at my side, taking my arm and tucking it under his elbow. I wondered that he had the nerve! At our last meeting he had accused Tristan of horrible things as well as snooping through my private belongings.

"Elinor, I've been waiting for you to emerge for over an hour."

I cast him a sideways glare. "You could have come up and paid a formal call. Or are you too ashamed?"

"Of what? Of doing my duty?" He might have said this blithely, but his eyes refused to meet mine. He nodded in a greeting at someone who passed us, but I wasn't going to let this slide. "Which begs the question that I wanted to ask you. I still don't understand why you were with de Windt at Hightower? I thought General Hatchet was your superior?"

"Not Hatchet, Axe. General Reynard 'Axe' Somerville. Yes, I was his attaché. Last month, they reassigned me to de Windt. You'd know if you read my letters."

"I do read your letters! But I've had a few things happening of late so I just forgot. I hadn't heard of de Windt until he showed up at Hightower."

Jacques, in his uniform with his height, athletic build, and handsome face, drew plenty of attention. As usual, he didn't seem to notice their admiration. Perhaps I should have felt smug being on his arm, but I felt only impatience.

"De Windt isn't military and from your uniform, you still are. So why are you with him?" I pressed.

"I was supposed to do a tour of duty with his department, and report back to Somerville my thoughts on the man. City crime is the provenance of the gendarmes, managed by the city government, but crimes against the king are the business of the Crown prosecutor. De Windt heads His Majesty's law enforcement branch, which means he can use the army as his enforcers.

Someone told him I knew you, and before I could pull on my boots, I was told to report for duty."

"Do you know who said you knew me?" I raised my eyebrows, waiting.

"It was some Society woman named Baudelaire."

"Hm." I was not feeling kindly towards my childhood chum, but if these were orders from a superior, he had no choice as an officer but to obey. I could not blame him for his actions at Hightower.

We said nothing for a few minutes, walking along the black railing along the canal. Finally, I broke the silence.

"You went back with de Windt and the duke, so perhaps you know what happened to Lady Tremblay?"

"House arrest for now. That doctor is missing, but her maid, who nursed Lord Tremblay, gave the same tale as her mistress. The doctor prescribed that so-called medicine which kept him going past his expiration date."

"What do you think will happen to her?"

He shrugged. Clearly, he was not concerned about her fate, which irritated me further. "Most likely released. I don't see how they can put her on trial. An aristo woman in the dock because her husband was a walking dead man? How would the charge of murder work?"

For the first time, I noticed there were no barges passing us by. Only the ducks were on the water today, and half of the shops along the river front were closed. Before I could think upon the why of this, Jacques interrupted my reverie. "You need to watch your step, Elinor."

"It seems a week of warnings," I replied mildly.

"De Windt seems to think you are conspiring with the Duke de Archambeau. He loathes Archambeau and is determined to cause you as much trouble as he can as the duke's ally."

"Why is that? Do you know?"

"Politics. He wants the prestige Archambeau has, the king's ear. It helps him feel righteous because of the duke's reputation."

I replied angrily, "What if I am working with Tristan? It's not any of his affair."

Jacques came to a halt. He grabbed my upper arm and squeezed, while saying harshly, "You little fool! It is exactly his affair! If King Guénard tells him to execute the duke de Archambeau or throw him down into an oubliette, he will do it! De Windt does what the king tells him to do. That is his job. Are you so infatuated that you don't understand the situation you are in? These are deep matters! Far too deep for a girl like you."

Facing him, I snapped back, "Deep matters? An innocent man is being chased by a bunch of cowardly hounds and you think I'll step back and let that happen? I once thought well of you, but you are like the rest of them. You are the one who is the fool! Blinded by prejudice. You've always had it in for him, Jacques. From the very beginning!"

His arm dropped, and we both took a step back, putting more distance between us. "I am not the fool here, Elinor. He deserves all that is said about him."

"Always with the vague hints," I sneered. "Perhaps you should tell me, or do you think I'm too much of a girl?"

He grimaced, looking away. "I knew his wife back in the day."

"Yes, you told me that. When I was in school, before my father died."

"There's more to it than that. When my tour was done, I came back to Alenbonné again. You were off with the Morpheus Society then so you wouldn't know, but we renewed our acquaintance as if I had never left. As if she had not married."

My eyebrows rose, for the implication was clear. "How could you? A married woman?"

"How could I not? She was so beautiful. A man ached to be in the same room as her, let alone touch her," he said, but his tone held rue and pain. He might defend her, but the relationship had hurt him. *This woman left a path of destruction behind her!*

"You don't understand—"

"What do I not understand? That you couldn't resist temptation?"

He started walking again, and I fell into step beside him. "I admit we enjoyed a flirtation, but I always knew she was above my reach. These nobles are very free and easy with love in their high-flying circles. They change beds at a whim, exchanging lovers like others do clothes. So I thought it was hopeless until—"

I asked, "What changed?"

"When I returned from some assignment on the border with a medal on my chest and landed a plum position working for Axe. I was at some party for the high-ups and I found her crying in a dark room. She was now married, but very unhappy."

He told me a tale of woe: of how Tristan hit and abused her; the tyranny she lived under in his house. I could even picture the scene in my mind's eye: the clasped hands beseeching his aid, the low-cut gown artfully arranged which showed her creamy breasts off to advantage, the tousled hair falling down her bare back, the eyes filled with tears that never spilled. *How I hated her!*

"And you believed that!?"

"Of course I did, because it was the truth. She had bruises on her. In places only her husband could have caused."

For a moment, he had me speechless. "When you became lovers, you saw these bruises?" His red face confirmed it. "Did it never occur to you that her other bedmates perhaps made those injuries?"

He reared back, affronted. "She said it was Tristan Fontaine and I believe her. After all, Elinor, she's the one dead, not him."

Yes, she was dead, and Tristan had killed her. Still, I did not believe the story she had told Jacques for one minute.

"She wasn't the innocent you thought, Jacques. Her class thinks nothing of taking lovers, but an affair with someone so junior in standing would never have been supported. It begs the question of why she seduced you."

"It was love. Passion. Sometimes class transcends these things, and it proves my argument that she must have really cared for me." His brain desperately wanted the words his tongue spoke to be true.

I hated to tell my old friend unpleasant truths, but delusion would not serve him. "Perhaps she did care for you, but don't you find it interesting that only after you became Somerville's attaché did this flirtation turn into an affair?"

He winced. "Do you not think I've considered that? Still, you didn't know her, Elinor. What we had. It was sincere. There is an honesty found in intimacy that someone as inexperienced as you cannot understand."

"She sold state secrets. Did she get that information from you?"

"No!" he cried. "The person who sold our country's secrets was the duke de Archambeau."

His accusation against Tristan made me go on the attack. "You know I'm right, don't you, Jacques? You gave her that information during some pillow talk. Later, she accused Tristan as the culprit to divert attention from the real person. You."

He pulled away, his back stiff, his face fixed in horror. "You're wrong, Elinor. You've got it backwards."

"Have I?"

"His Grace is the traitor! He blames her for his own crimes. She was the victim, not him!"

I grabbed his arm, stopping him from leaving. "Ask yourself why a social climber like Minette Fontaine stooped to take a baseborn lover? It goes against the creed of her class. What were you doing for the general, Jacques, when you 'accidentally' found her playing a helpless victim? What secrets did you know back then?"

He shook me off, now furious. "You didn't know her! It is easy to accuse her in order to salve your own conscience. Good luck to you Elinor. You will need it when your highborn lover falls."

He turned sharply on his boot heel, fists clenched at his side, back unbending, as he marched away. It was done with the precision of the soldier on parade. I had never seen him so angry with me before. Had I destroyed our long friendship? I did not regret my words, but was I right? Where had Minette gotten the secrets she had sold? From Tristan's desk or Jacques' mouth?

"Madame Chalamet."

The voice behind me made me jump. My hand instinctively went into my dress pocket, where my fingers folded around the smooth handle of my gun.

"Who are you?" Standing with the sun behind him for a moment, the man's bulk made me think of Sergeant Dupont, but as he moved closer, I saw that he was a much younger man. About the size of the sergeant, along with the strong muscular build of a man who worked the docks or wrestled for a living. But his hair was white-blond and his face round and smooth.

"I didn't mean to alarm you, madame." He took off his hat and held it in hands that could have easily crushed a melon. "The duke de Archambeau sent me to look after you."

"Look after me?"

"I'm here to make sure no one bothers you. I would suggest you return to the hotel. It's not a good day for a woman to be out alone."

My shoulders heaved with a sigh. I might want to forget my life was under threat, but it seemed Tristan would not.

"No insult intended, but how do I know that the duke sent you?"

He handed me a piece of folded paper. Inside was Tristan's scrawl: *You refuse to be cautious, so these two shall keep you safe despite yourself.*

Refolding it, I slipped it into a pocket. I asked, "What is your name?"

"Farrow. You'll meet my fellow guard, Styles, tomorrow. We will hang back and not interfere with your daily regime. I assure you we can be discreet. But it would be best if we can arrange some signal to know when you want us by your side. You seemed friendly enough with that fellow in the beginning, but it didn't look like a conversation you were enjoying by the end."

I sighed. "Jacques is a childhood friend. Sometimes we argue. Should I have shouted for help if he had been a problem?"

"Perhaps something more subtle for those times when you only need us to show our presence. Most of these villains will take off running when they know a lady has a man at her call."

While I would rather take care of myself, Mysir Farrow had a good point. His physical presence was imposing. "I shall first touch my throat and then adjust my hat." Performing the gestures as described, he nodded his understanding. "I appreciate His Grace looking after me, but I will be about my business and not hiding in my hotel room."

"The streets are not as safe as you may think," was his only comment.

"Then it is fortunate you will be about."

CHAPTER FIVE

T he next evening Tristan was right on time, impeccably tailored as usual. It was almost enough to make a girl want to check her hair in a mirror. I tucked my hand within the crook of his arm and told Anne-Marie she could go on home.

As we made our way down the grand staircase of the Crown hotel, we turned a few heads. Tristan was far better at pretending no one else existed, but I felt my cheeks grow warm at the attention and was thankful when the door to his carriage closed behind us. It was the anonymous one without his coat of arms on the door.

Seating himself next to me, he said, "Now, don't be angry with me, but Valentina will be meeting us at the theater." Perhaps it was the expression on my face which had him add hastily, "She won't be with us for dinner, though."

"Your sister? Why?" It was hard to keep the disappointment from my voice. Were we never to be alone? Just the two of us without an interruption or a watcher?

"Trust me, it surprised me, too. When she discovered I was using our box this evening with you, she insisted on coming to see *Love Lacks a Lady*."

Did Valentina think we needed a guardian?

"Have the two of you discussed the king's letters?"

"No."

It seemed he didn't want to discuss the matter further, so I set my irritation aside. I didn't want the evening spoiled. Tristan had booked a dinner reservation at the Charmont, a place I had been dying to try. It was horrendously expensive, and so exclusive I had avoided the place. Now, with someone else paying the tab, I was curious to see what I had missed.

The outside of the building was subdued and nondescript, with the brick painted black and the windows heavily curtained. At the door there were two gaslamps, one on either side, which cast a flickering light under the portico. Only a very small sign at the door stated the name of the establishment.

It all looked subdued and commonplace, or very secretive and exclusive. Sometimes extravagance translated itself to simplicity.

"This is it?" I asked when the carriage stopped in front of it.

Tristan chuckled. "Come along, madame, and you'll see."

A butler ushered us in, quickly taking Tristan's top hat and scarf. I decided to keep my fur around my bare shoulders.

The interior walls of the Charmont were all painted a black-blue so dark that the hint of color on it was only revealed where candles flickered near it.

Following the butler, with Tristan's arm guiding me, we traveled through a maze of halls and past several curtained alcoves. Any diners at the open tables who saw us ignored us. In the end, our table was in a half-concealed alcove where a crescent-shaped booth seat covered in aquamarine velvet was positioned so deeply in its interior that those seated would be removed from casual view. Drapes on either side could be drawn to give us absolute privacy.

Yes, the plain exterior had hidden an interior that whispered exclusive and private. I was glad I wasn't the one paying the tab tonight. After the maitre d' left, I whispered to Tristan, "This looks like a place men bring their mistresses to."

Without missing a beat, he replied, "It's where they bring someone they want to impress."

"Oh? Do you think it can do so for someone who dines daily on the offerings of Chef Perdersen?" I asked loftily.

"Wait and see." He gave me a knowing smile.

There was no menu card or selection to be made. Tristan explained that what we were served was at the discretion of the chef, who would decide what he would send. In total silence, our waiter set down an ice bucket with a bottle and left again. The wine was Chambaux. Pouring it out, Tristan said blandly, "I hope you like this vintage."

"I like everything that comes from Chambaux," I replied with a smirk, which elicited a gravelly chuckle from him. Gazing down on the white tablecloth with more silver than a king's treasure room, I commented in awe, "I've never seen so many spoons and knives."

"It does look a bit extravagant. However, I doubt in this candlelight anyone will know if we choose the wrong one."

"I can't imagine you stepping wrong— it will be poor me using the wrong spoon, you'll see."

Perhaps he saw my double meaning, for he said more seriously, "I don't care about spoons, Elinor. And if anyone else passing our table has a derogatory comment about your choice, they shall find their nose bloodied."

"Why be so severe? Just freeze them with one of your glares."

"I do not glare."

"Yes, you do."

We were both laughing when the first course of soup arrived. If I had thought Chef Perdersen was a marvel, he paled compared to the genius ruling the Charmont kitchen.

The portions were small, and I soon realized why. There was a never-ending stream of taste sensations for the diner to experience. Each gave an incredibly nuanced set of flavors which I had never tasted before; the combinations were intriguing and unusual, yet pleasant. There was a mini cup of sorbet to serve as a palate cleanser between courses.

Tristan gave a rueful laugh. "If only I could bring that look upon your face, Elinor."

I opened my eyes. "But have you tried this lobster?"

"Of course. I finished it about ten minutes ago."

"Good things are meant to be savored."

At the end, we were brought tiered serving trays filled with petit fours. The silent server untied the drapes and with a whisper of silk they closed, leaving us private.

It all felt very wicked, and I blushed furiously under Tristan's gaze. Perhaps he saw that as an invitation, for he edged closer and ran his finger under the strap of my gown on my left shoulder, causing it to fall down.

"I recognize this dress," he murmured.

"You should. You paid for it, thinking I would become your mistress."

"It was a wise investment, even though you didn't take me up on the offer. You look ravishing in it."

"I didn't know there was an offer!"

He drew closer, and his arm went around the back of the seat. His fingers lightly caressed the nape of my neck, making me shiver all the way to my slippers. "How did you like your gift, madame?"

"I spent the day unlocking everything I could find. But one is giving me trouble."

The hand not drawing whisper-soft loops on my neck picked up one of mine in order to examine my fingers. I think my hand trembled. "Perhaps you need my assistance. Locks can be very tricky things sometimes."

"I do like things that are hard to figure out," I confided.

He bent his head, and his lips grazed my exposed shoulder. His lips murmured against my skin, "You are the only puzzle I wish to unlock. How you think. What you want." His hand moved, grazing where my father's watch marked me. A mark that only he and Leona Granger could see.

Concerned, he asked, "Has this not gone away? Have you seen Dr. LaRue about it?"

"It's nothing," I murmured, not wanting to discuss it.

He kissed it, setting me to trembling. He brought me closer and nibbled the lobe of my ear, making me squeak. Then he had to spoil it all.

"Elinor, will you marry me?"

I jerked in his arms, alarmed. "No. That's impossible."

"Many things are possible that you would think otherwise. And this seems rather a simple thing to handle since it only requires filing for a license and an officiate."

"You know it's not that simple! We're from two different worlds. It wouldn't work out in the long run. What would your mother, your sister, your friends think of you?"

His expression was hard to interpret. I tried explaining what had been bothering me since leaving Hightower. "I love you, Tristan, but I can't be the hostess of Hartwood House. Imagine me as the Duchesse de Chambaux! I'd be horrid at it and embarrass you at every turn."

"I think the Chambaux name can handle you, forgetting which spoon to use."

I protested, almost crying, "But could I handle it? The ridicule because of my station in life? Before I met you, I was unaware my position in life was so repellent to so many people."

"You mean the Le beau idéal," he said dismissively. "We can ignore them. They don't matter."

He was willfully refusing to understand. "You can ignore them because you belong to it. But what about me? What about your mother?"

He frowned. "Well, she won't be happy, but she had her say with my first marriage. Besides, it might surprise you to find support from another quarter. My sister, I think, would be your ally."

"Valentina?" I cried, astonished.

"When she came back from Hightower, she didn't exactly sing your praises, but she did advise me to pay you a call. From her, that is practically a signed endorsement."

Did she think this would pay me back for what I had done for her at Hightower and the beach? I did not want her approval at such a cost, and shook my head. "Really, Tristan, you must see it would never work. I'm too outspoken, too independent. I like my own way, and would make a horrible wife for you."

"I've had a horrible wife before, Elinor. I doubt you could match her." His arm dropped from my waist, although he still stayed close. "Stubborn, Elinor. That's the word you are looking for to describe yourself. Any other woman would be asking to set the date."

"Have you ever thought about how much I would need to give up? My profession as a Ghost Talker? Coming and going as I pleased? Having my own friends, my money? Is it wrong for me to have my life the way I want it?"

"I do not see how these things would have to change if you wore my ring."

"Oh, Tristan. Think!"

"This perfect life of yours? How do I fit into that? Or do I?" he said, cynically.

"Why is everything so complicated?" I cried, feeling tears spring to my eyes. "Why can't we enjoy this? Whatever *this* is without the need for labels that society makes us use."

"Because I love you, Elinor. I want you as my partner, help-mate, and lover. By my side, always. Not living at the Crown, seeing each other in passing. I want our lives to be one, not two."

"As sweet as those words are, if we married, it would be I who would lose status. I'd be your second, lesser-than, easy-to-dispose-of-wife. If you ever took the fancy to get rid of me, the courts would not object."

I only realized after the words left my mouth that he would take it to mean how had Minette died, but I couldn't stop my misstep. My heart was beating like I had run a race. Things were crashing down and coming to an end.

"Or worse, you'd keep me, but take a mistress, a woman higher in rank."

His features became set and remote. "So, how do you see this working? You prefer to be my mistress? All the money, but none of the grief?"

"No! I don't want to be a mistress or wife. Only me! Only us. Right at this moment. Why can't this be enough?" I begged.

It seemed he had no answer for me. Drawing back, he stood up.

"We best be going if we are to make the theater in time."

CHAPTER SIX

There were three major theaters and one opera house in Alenbonné. Of the three theaters, one had burned down last summer, and the famous actor, Bartel Kingma, had perished. I raised my hand in passing, sending him a silent thanks for helping me with Lady Annabel van den Berg last night.

The silence in the carriage was like burning ice, so I was relieved when the carriage pulled up to the steps of the Luminary, a theater known for farces and clever plays that lampooned the latest society scandals by setting them all to scathing humor. It was immensely popular, which made me wonder if the nobility it satirized fully understood what they were watching.

I hoped tonight's offering was funny because the carriage ride had decidedly not been. My expectations of a pleasurable seduction, to which I was ready to put up a token resistance, were turned upside down. Kisses would have been so much more agreeable than an unwanted marriage proposal!

Etiquette demanded that we enter arm in arm, but Tristan's was stiff and unyielding. The lobby had a crimson carpet with velvet drapes and gilt mirrors reflecting the light of electric chandeliers. The Luminary was in the middle of transitioning from gas to electric and the change was impressive.

There was quite a crowd making the area warm. In the foyer, ladies were gently fanning themselves while gentlemen tried hard to impress them with their mustaches and stories. Perhaps people were tired of being stuck at home, for there were more than I had expected.

If heads did not turn, eyes did, and I felt a series of pinpricks down my spine. Being in a public place with the Duke de Archambeau raised the attention of gossips. Stupidly, I had not foreseen this outing gaining me the very interest I wanted to avoid. Keeping my love affair private while enjoying Tristan's company was proving difficult.

We found Lady Valentina Fontaine waiting for us. Her companion showed me the evening was quickly going from bad to worse.

"Jacques!" I said, exclaimed in a voice that was not enthusiastic. After our last discussion, and in my current mood, I was not pleased with his appearance. I couldn't imagine why he was here and in company with Tristan's sister.

"Elinor," he returned, giving us a stiff bow.

Jacques, the former lover of my lover's wife. The whole thing smacked of a farce. We should get on stage and play it out for an audience.

Lady Valentina gave an explanation that I did not believe. "When I accidentally met Mysir Moreau at a friend's luncheon, I thought you might like to visit with your childhood friend. He makes our party an even number."

The men viewed each other with the aspect of two tom cats who had met in an alley by mischance. Before I could think of anything to say to calm the waters, there was another disaster to sour what had started out a promising evening.

Behind me a familiar and hateful voice said in an affected drawl, "How delightful to see you, dear Valentina. I did not think you were in town since you were not at home when I called earlier today."

Practiced in all the social graces, Valentina needed only a moment before issuing a polite pleasantry. "There is always so much to do when one returns to town. Josephine. I do not know if you have met my companion, Jacques Moreau? Lady Josephine Baudelaire."

Josephine gave that twittering artificial laugh. "Oh, we met long ago. Through Minette. She always introduced me to all of her personal friends."

At this statement, both men became as immobile as statues, leaving the ladies to do the heavy lifting.

I replied, "Lady Baudelaire, how delightful to see you again so soon. Is that dress by the modiste you told us about? How beautiful. But certainly it would perfectly showcase your husband's family heirloom? That necklace I saw you wear at the dinner held at Hartwood where we met? I believe those diamonds would be the perfect complement to your icy blue gown."

To give the woman her due, she showed no response to my remark about a family heirloom that had been recently found in a blackmailer's safe. It confirmed my opinion that I would not want to play cards with her, for her face would reveal nothing. Perhaps it had set in one position so subtleties were now difficult for it to produce?

She ignored my comment and addressed Tristan's sister again. "You must come by this week to help me pick the music for my soirée. You have such excellent taste, Valentina, and it will give us time for a long private chat that is much overdue."

Tristan finally awoke from his angry stupor and said in that tone that brooked no argument, "Unfortunately, my sister shall not have time for such a visit. She is leaving tomorrow for Chambaux at the request of our mother."

I could tell from Valentina's blink that such a request had never happened. However, she recovered quickly. "It is almost time for the harvest and Mother is always involved, despite our cousin managing the summer workers."

"Perhaps it would be best if her son and heir would attend to managing his vast estate. I am sure His Majesty would gladly spare him," said Josephine waspishly.

I wasn't sure that Tristan needed any defense from me, especially after our argument over dinner, but that didn't stop me from trying.

"I'm afraid he could not. King Guénard relies on him. Only yesterday, during our tête-à-tête, His Majesty lamented about the falseness of court sycophants. He has so many liars around him who bear false tales, you see. People who like to stir up trouble give him quite a headache."

I wished I could tell her that the king had given Tristan permission to make her vanish, but there was no way to work that into a polite conversation.

I asked Valentina, "Were you at Lady Annabel van den Berg's birthday celebration last night? It was so entertaining. A ghostly admirer appeared and apologized for how his possessive jealousy made him push her down the stairs. He declared his undying love and begged her forgiveness. It was all very romantic."

Josephine's face went through several transformations as I spoke. First, her condescending sneer froze; next her eyes widened, and her skin went pale under her makeup; and finally, she moved her gaze to across the room to avoid meeting our eyes.

Her eyes fastened upon Lady Annabel who was holding court with a group of young men. She had already pointed her fan twice in my direction while talking excitedly. I was pretty sure that the gossip about my visit to her home was rapidly being spread.

Recovering with some difficulty, Josephine said to Tristan's sister, "I hope you enjoy the play before you run back to Chambaux, Valentina. Now, if you will excuse me?"

The men gave her a brief bow, and I saw her weaving through

the crowd, making her way slowly over to where Lady van den Berg stood.

Good. Let her find out that her scheming had failed. She had no hold over Valentina any more since no one would believe a story about trip wire when a love-lorn ghost lover was a far more exciting story. Besides, Lady Annabel herself attested to it being true.

Staring after her, I heard Tristan say with some amusement, "Come along, Elinor, before you take down any more of my enemies."

Of course, the Chambaux family had a reserved box. He escorted me up the stairs while Jacques guided Valentina. It was the closest to the stage and gave us a prime view. We found our seats: first Valentina, then Jacques, myself, and Tristan at the opposite end of the row.

Below us others were trickling down the aisle. Valentina pulled out a pair of small binoculars from her beaded bag and brought them to her eyes to scan the venue. Whether we wanted to know, she started telling us who she saw.

"That review in the *Tattletale* must have brought out all the season ticket-holders. Lord and Lady Dorenkamp. I'm surprised to see her considering her delicate condition. We must remember to send her some fruit, Tristan. Isn't that your General Somerville, Mysir Moreau? Who is that lady sitting next to him?"

Jacques looked where she pointed and told her, "That's his lady wife, Madame Venetia. She loves the theater, but I will lay you a royal that he falls asleep before the end of the first act."

"I see the king's ward, Lady Tulip Langenberg with that strange man we met at the Winter Revels. What is his name again?"

I supplied it. "Theodore Visscher. He's a professor I believe at the university. Or a student. Maybe both."

"Very handsome. Do we know who his family is?"

Still looking down at his program, Tristan answered her. "Visscher is a scion of the Groendyke estate, which is not impoverished, but not rich. Their heir should stick to teaching and not meddle in matters that could be poor for his continuing health."

I wanted to know what Tristan meant by that statement, but now was not the time to ask. Valentina's roving attention was still combing the room. "There does seem to be a vast number of the nobility here. And some of those government officials you've brought around so much. Like that woman there. Lady Maryegold Talleyrand, isn't it? Or do my eyes betray me?"

"Your eyes, looking through those binoculars, never betray you, Valentina," said Tristan sarcastically. "Yes, it is her. I'm not surprised she wants some time away from arguing with those knuckleheads in parliament."

"Oh, what does she do there?" I asked, curious about the role of a woman in the government.

"She's one of the few women who serve in the House of Lords," Tristan explained. He put aside his program to look down to where Lady Talleyrand sat.

"She's a born diplomat, and the only person I've ever seen who could get His Majesty to actually listen and change his mind. We are lucky to have her. Especially during these turbulent times."

She didn't seem very special on the outside: a middle-aged woman, wearing a deep blue satin dress that was neither too high fashion nor too low. Perfectly respectable, but more understated than what I thought a high society lady would usually wear. Her white hair was not in an elaborate style but swept up smoothly from the side to a coil in the back. I did not have Valentina's binoculars, but my sharp eyes saw she wore pearls and diamonds in a set that matched her earrings.

Her companion was a younger woman dressed in a more youthful fashion of alternating stripes of pink and fuchsia. She wore only a gold chain with a locket around her neck. She was very attentive to the older lady, and I guessed her to be a relation.

The lights flickered, and it was time to put away the glasses and our curiosity. While the lobby had electric lighting, the stage used the older gaslamps at the front of the stage to illuminate the actors. The orchestra changed their tune to something brighter and as the stage curtains were being pulled up with golden ropes.

It was an enjoyable play with good acting and funny lines, but my mind kept replaying the scene at dinner. I couldn't quite see Tristan spending his day at the Crown while I talked with ghosts. Meanwhile, the idea of hosting a society party at Hartwood House made my soul shrink.

There must be a way to work things out! After all, we were two intelligent people. Somehow Tristan and I were going to make this work and all would be well, I assured myself.

Tristan needed me. When he'd thought I was scheming with the king, he had been genuinely disturbed. He was more vulnerable to hurt than I expected, and although he hid it well, the blows could hurt. There was more to him than the label of the Duke de Archambeau.

Catching my thoughtful glance, he asked, "What are you staring at?"

I mouthed back, "You."

He reached over and covered my hand. "Forgiven?"

"Perhaps it is you who should forgive me?"

"I'm sure I was in the wrong, wanting you to spend the rest of your life with me," he said, with only a hint of sarcasm in his words.

Before I could respond, I realized that the raucous shouting I had mistaken for part of the play was actually a group marching down the aisle holding signs above their head. Something stirred inside me. Without thinking, I stood up, my hands on the balcony as I looked down at the newcomers.

Jacques muttered under his breath, "Damn protesters! They're everywhere!" Embarrassed by his language, he quickly added, "Pardon, Lady Fontaine."

However, Lady Valentina wasn't paying attention to him. She was staring over Jacques's shoulder directly at me. "Elinor, do you know you're glowing?"

CHAPTER SEVEN

Valentina had her mouth half open, her brow slightly furrowed as her puzzled eyes stared at me. Jacques was still gazing down over the balcony to the crowd below us, while Tristan had his head cocked, paused in mid-turn.

Like the day on the beach, dreamlike, time for everyone else seemed to have slowed. I felt a heaviness in my chest, right above my heart. The air was oppressive, smothering me as the precognitive images started.

A nightmare unfolded of what could be. The shouting protesters pushed past the ushers who tried to restrain them, but their words were gibberish and held no meaning.

The group was of older men and women. All mature, with many having white or graying hair. The men wore shabby coats of brown and gray, and a few were barefoot. The women were not much better, but a few had faded shawls wrapped tightly around their shoulders which they clenched closed with bony fingers.

They were from the streets: the poorest class of vagrants, streetwalkers, thieves, and beggars. And I knew in my heart they were only shells, devoid of intelligence or life. While Gilbert Tremblay had been alive enough for his energy not to betray him to eyes used to communing with the dead, these creatures were closer to being corpses. Their bodies moving like stringed puppets.

And there were so many of them, all in one place.

The problem with a polite society is that when faced with the unusual, they become dumbstruck and slow to respond to anything outrageous. At first the audience remained seated, their conversation only murmurs. These new arrivals puzzled them. Were they part of the play? Part of the entertainment?

The players on stage started shouting at the newcomers to leave, and the theater manager came out to bring order. The audience began to realize that these people were not actors, but invaders.

Lady Talleyrand rose to leave, her young companion accompanying her. She must have come with a party of several men, who rose at the same time and helped her make it to the end of the aisle. By surrounding her, they could push through and get her to the doors that exited to the lobby.

Others were not as fortunate.

An audience member, a man with black hair and a thick mustache, rose from his seat in the front row as if to leave, but a newcomer shoved him back down. Angered, the man jumped back up from his seat again and swung a punch at the protester, who fell heavily backward.

He tumbled into a woman vagrant. She gave an inhuman shriek, throwing her hands up in an attempt to keep her balance. The shawl on her shoulders dropped away, fluttering behind her like a sail, and the tail of it crossed over one of the open gas jets that illuminated the stage. To my horror, the flames raced up her shawl and leaped onto her dress, transforming her into a human torch.

The audience screamed and scrambling to their feet, trying to gain the exit. But they were too late. Silk and cotton begged to be on fire and summer dresses were the perfect fuel.

I gasped, bringing my fist to my mouth as I watched it unfold.

No. I would need to stop that from happening. I shook my head, throwing away the precognitive dream state.

Time returned to now, and I heard Valentina's question. "Elinor, do you know you're glowing?"

I ignored her and grabbed Tristan's arm, shaking it hard. "The protesters— they are the dead-alive! Like Lord Tremblay! They will cause a fire from the gaslights on the stage! The theater is in danger."

He asked me no silly questions such as how I knew this, but understood immediately the gravity of the situation and sprang into decisive action.

"Get down there to the manager," he ordered Jacques. "Have him shut down those gaslights on stage. Now! By the order of His Majesty!"

Orders were something Jacques understood. Without hesitation, he threw one leg over the balcony and grabbed a fistful of velvet drape as Valentina gasped.

"I think I'll take the quickest route down," he told her with a grin.

Before we could protest, he was over the edge, climbing down the drapes even as they ripped from the rod that hung from above. He rode the momentum to the floor. On stage, he jumped over to where the manager was shouting at the protesters. Grabbing the man he shouted at him to turn off the gas.

In the audience, Lady Talleyrand was rising from her seat, just as she had in my dream. The gas needed to be shut off before what I foresaw became reality!

Tristan grabbed his sister by her arm and, telling me to follow, dragged her out towards the stairs. Valentina asked questions all the way.

"What is this about Lord Tremblay? Why is Elinor glowing? Will someone please explain to me what is going on?"

We had no time to answer.

In the lobby, Tristan issued orders to the theater staff, who were milling about in confusion. "Open the doors! All of you, start evacuating the theater." Someone must have protested, because I heard Tristan shout angrily, "Do you want them dead!? Because that is what will happen if they stay here. Get them out! Now!"

The theater seated at least one hundred. While most of the audience goers were leaving under the command of the ushers, some seemed to think the entire thing was amusing. They stayed, pointing at the protesters waving their signs, and laughed.

I heard Tristan mutter, "Idiots. At this rate, they'll never get out of here in time."

The electric over our head flickered and went out, while the stage remained brightly lit. I moaned in dismay. They had turned out the electric but not the gas.

In the turmoil, the souls of the four girls that Parnell Lafayette had used to build his palace in the Beyond, and who had helped me Sunder the soul of the killer Vonn, stirred. In my heart they played their music: flute, harp, cello, and violin. Their melody started to drown out the noises in the theater. The four pulled at me, demanding attention with their siren music.

My head started to hurt, and lights flashed before my eyes. I staggered, only to feel Tristan's firm grip on my elbow, holding me upright. "You and Valentina should leave."

Collapsing against him, I could only gasp out, "The Beyond" before my mind whirled away to elsewhere.

The sounds of the protesters, the smell of the theater was gone, and I stood alone in a misty gray land where ghosts ruled. A place I had avoided since my final confrontation with Parnell Lafayette.

For a moment I stood there stunned trying to puzzle out what had brought me here. Of course— the soul sisters. Why? And why now?

I covered my nose. What was that horrible reek? I could smell the suffocating stench of the dead. *Impossible! That can not be!* Something was wrong. Dreadfully wrong. The Beyond was a null world of shadows and did not carry the liveliness of the real world.

Four pillars, the souls of the dead girls who were now always with me. They surrounded me in a protective circle, preventing me from moving.

Through the bars, I now saw the dead-alive souls of those people I had glimpsed in the theater. These creatures must be close to death and trapped by their bodies, from continuing their journey to the Afterlife.

Suspended between life and death, unable to move on to the Afterlife, they existed in an unnatural suspension of the cycle of life. Seeing me, they crowded forward, shouting at me, "Save us. Save our souls! We live in torment! Bring us peace."

Only the pillars of gold light prevented them from touching me. I shrank back from the onslaught as they pressed closer, their hands trying to reach through my protective gold shield.

The only way I knew to help them would be through a Sundering, something I had done to Vonn using the energy from the four dead girls he had held captive in the Beyond. It was how they had become bonded to me, but could I use them again? And should I? For if I did a Sundering, it would destroy these people's souls on all three planes. Their chance of redemption lost.

Besides, it was a monumental task, and I did not think I was up to doing it again, emotionally or physically. And for so many? Impossible!

The music of flute, harp, cello, and violin flowed together, reaching a harmony of a tune I had never heard before. Then suddenly one became louder, drowning out the rest: the violin.

One of the four gold columns pulled away. As she left me it felt like a birth, letting a part of me— a part separate from me— leave. The severing of our connection made me gasp in pain. My heart felt on fire and my hand went up to clutch over the area of my breast where my father's watch had marked me. I tried to suck in air and found myself unable to breathe.

She had a name: Frida Korver. No longer a gold pillar, she once again took human form, the shape of the statue I had seen in

Parnell's palace. Still gold, but she had a face with a nose, eyes, and mouth. Arms and legs.

She stood in profile, the form of a young girl shaped in golden light, her figure translucent as people thought ghosts were. Frida was perhaps fourteen, no more than sixteen, with a triangular face and eyes that should laugh, not be gold and inhuman like they were now. Her liquid gold hair was long and tied back with a ribbon, signifying that she had been a girl still in the schoolroom when Parnell had ensnared her in his scheme.

Damn him. Where had he found this innocent child?

I reached out, but she moved further away, and the three remaining gold soul sisters wrapped around me tightly, preventing me from following. I could only watch.

Frida was moving among the dead-alive. They parted, making way for her, silent but watching her. Then they started to crowd around her, blocking her from my view, their voices coming together as one chorus.

"Save us! Save our souls!"

Even as I screamed her name, a shaft of light like a train's headlight pierced the gray sky above. Then it collapsed, falling back down in a shower of sparkling gold drops which rained down on these trapped souls. As the gold touched them, they dissolved, melting into nothingness, but from the center, a whirlwind grew. It spun faster and faster, whipping my garments around my body, tearing my hair from its pins.

A burst of wind threw me backward and a spray of rainbow light blinded me as I fell and fell and fell.

CHAPTER EIGHT

I awoke lying on a red carpet, something stinging my nostrils. Coughing, I tried to sit up, but a hand kept me down.

"Damn you, Elinor. Are you determined to frighten me to death?"

I blinked rapidly, trying to bring things back into focus. Tristan, the Duke de Archambeau, was leaning over me and his sister, Lady Valentina, was kneeling beside me holding a bottle of smelling salts. It was a scene odder than watching lost souls go to the Afterlife.

"Elinor? How do you feel?" was his sister's gentler inquiry.

I tried again to sit up, and this time Valentina assisted me, shooting a sideways look at her brother. I mumbled, "What happened?"

"You mean after you collapsed and your heart stopped beating?" snapped Tristan sarcastically. He was towering over me. I wanted to tell him to stop behaving like a child who had lost its lolly, but my body hurt too much to make the effort.

Valentina explained. "Jacques got the gaslights turned off and then you fainted. A few moments later, the rioters in the theater fell to the ground."

"No one got hurt, did they?" I didn't mean the dead-alives, of course.

"No one but you, you silly fool," said Tristan, still angry.

I regained my feet, but before I could topple over again, Tristan swept me up in his arms. As he carried me through the lobby, I caught sight of some familiar faces: Lady Tulip, who was standing next to Mysir Vischeer; Josephine Baudelaire, and Annabel van den Berg.

Outside, the night air was a relief to my aching head. People in fancy dress were talking to gendarmes in their uniforms of navy blue with red trim and flat hats.

"Valentina, the door," said Tristan sternly. His sister, who had been following us, hurried forward and opened the carriage door. Tristan set me gently down on the seat and I leaned back into the corner, feeling the sides of it like an embrace.

In a small voice, I said, "My heart really didn't stop beating, did it?"

"Just rest, Elinor." Valentina took my fur and settled it around my chest, wrapping it around my neck.

My scattered thoughts were drifting. I tried to focus and asked in a weak voice, "When did the gendarmes arrive?"

"Too late, as always," said Tristan shortly. He was standing outside, his hand on the ledge of the carriage door as, frowning, he surveyed the crowd.

Valentina, who had settled across from me, patted my hand. "I believe an usher summoned them."

Behind Tristan, a familiar head appeared. It was Inspector Barbier.

"I hear you've had a bit of excitement," was his droll comment. Tristan didn't seem amused, but I spoke up.

"Just a little."

"We're waiting for the doctor to get here. Expect you'll want to talk with her."

Tristan stopped scanning the crowd and asked, "Dr. LaRue?"

"Yeah. I sent a carriage for her. Plenty blood and gore for her to sift through down there. I don't think there will be anything to Ghost Talk. Sorry, Elinor."

With their souls gone, I didn't think there would be any information.

"When the doctor gets here, send her to me first," said Tristan.

Barbier seemed surprised at the request but agreed to do so.

"Your Grace!" said a voice from a man pushing through the crowd, making me groan and sink back into the darkness of the carriage. It was Sven de Windt, the senior prosecutor for the Crown whom we had met at Hightower House. A man who wanted to believe Tristan was a traitor.

His appearance caused a ripple of tension between Tristan and Barbier. The inspector dropped his eyes to his open notebook, where he had been making notes with his pencil, clearly hoping not to be noticed. Tristan's grip on the carriage door made his knuckles whiten.

De Windt was in his official black uniform with its cuffs of scarlet and gold braid. Under his arm was tucked his flat cap. He had a thin face, a long nose, and eyes set too close together for my liking.

"Sven," Tristan greeted him before introducing the Crown prosecutor to the inspector. De Windt gave Barbier a throwaway nod before launching into demands that Tristan explain what had happened at the Luminary.

"Word came into my office that some radicals were down here, causing a disturbance. Are they arrested yet?"

I wasn't able to suppress a giggle, which made de Windt notice me, unfortunately.

Barbier flipped open his notebook and started reading them aloud. "It seems a group of anti-monarchists staged a protest at the Luminary. They've been holding these demonstrations for months now, growing ever bolder. A small group, usually less than twenty, shows up to an event where the nobility gather in order to harass them. Usually, it's just a nuisance that is quickly resolved; the rascals flee when my men arrive. Rabble, Mysir de Windt."

"Their riots are a bit more than that, Inspector Barbier," snapped de Windt. "There's been destruction of property, injuries, and a disruption of the king's peace. They are revolutionaries. Anarchists! They seek the end of our monarchy. A total disruption to the Sarnesse way of life."

Barbier picked a piece of lint from his brown wool lapel and flicked it away. "They may seek that, but it is unlikely they will find it."

Tristan interrupted them. "I would rather discuss what happened tonight. The play hadn't been going on long when this group entered the theater. I counted twelve. Three women and nine men, their ages close to fifty or sixty. They wore the garments of workers, cottons and linens, but still I thought their clothes were shabby even for that class."

Barbier took notes in his little book, jotting down Tristan's comments with his pencil.

"I had Jacques Moreau leave our box to warn the manager of the danger the gaslamps could present with such an unruly crowd. At my request, the ushers started to clear out the audience, for I feared people might panic and make the situation worse."

"Mysir Moreau was with you?" asked de Windt in a tone that didn't bode well for Jacques.

Valentina leaned out of the carriage window and said to him in a dulcet tone, "Oh dear, Mysir de Windt, that was by my invitation. But thank goodness he was with us, for he prevented the possibility of another theater fire like what happened at the Starlit."

At the mention of the theater that had burned to the ground killing eighteen people, de Windt softened somewhat. Or perhaps that was due to Valentina, who was using her aristo charm upon him?

"Well, then I'm glad that he was, even though he should have consulted with me first on his plans for the evening."

Tristan said in a lower voice that was probably meant not to be heard by the ladies in the group, "At one point, the protesters suddenly collapsed. Dead. Have you seen the bodies, de Windt? They are in the same state as our late Gilbert Tremblay."

De Windt's nose positively quivered at that information. "That is why we need to keep this situation under control. Prevent gossip as best as we can. I suggest we get the names of those that attended the play and send them home."

De Windt immediately gave orders to Barbier, "Send these people home and make sure you get rid of the actors and the stage crew. We don't want them in there mucking about with my evidence."

Barbier paused, giving de Windt a pregnant stare before snapping his notebook shut. "I was doing just that when you arrived, mysir." Without a goodbye, he turned on his heel to make his way back to where his men were. He seemed to dislike de Windt as much as I did.

De Windt spared a suspicious glance towards me. "What's she doing here?"

Tristan said stiffly, "Madame Chalamet attended the theater by my invitation."

"What does she have to say about this mess?" He waved his hand back towards the Luminary, taking in the theater. "What did she do?"

Before I could respond, Tristan name-dropped. "You might not be aware, but Lady Talleyrand and General Somerville were attending the play tonight."

That distracted de Windt from me, and his full attention swung upon Tristan. "Were they harmed?"

"To my knowledge, they are safe. Perhaps you should verify that?"

Unfortunately, de Windt did not take the hint and leave.

Instead, he stepped closer to Tristan and asked quietly, "What did you mean that these people were like Lord Tremblay? You aren't saying they were— What caused them to collapse, do you suppose?"

"Well, we know in Lord Tremblay's case it was because he had not received his daily elixir. Until we know more about these people, where they came from, who they were, I think we should not speculate." Tristan gave emphasis to the last three words, not looking in my direction. He wanted me to remain silent, and I was happy to oblige. I was exhausted.

"I see Dr. LaRue," he went on. "We can chat more about this later de Windt, but for now, I need to consult the doctor." He waited until de Windt left us and then turned to us in the carriage. "I'll be right back."

While we waited, Valentina hesitated before asking me, "What happened to the letters? Were you able to retrieve them?"

"Yes, and they are back in His Majesty's hands."

She exhaled a sigh of relief. "I wondered. Tristan has been acting strangely for the last day. I was worried you had told him of my involvement."

"Unfortunately, he does know. And about Lady Baudelaire's blackmail. I'm sorry. He found me with the king when I was returning the letters."

Her shoulders sagged. "Then I was right about his dark mood. He's been nothing but pleasant on the surface, but you can feel something under it all."

I reached over and squeezed her hand. "Do not worry. He knows you are not to blame and tried to hide them."

"Does he know about-?"

"No. And he won't unless you decide to tell him."

"Thank you, Elinor."

She seemed willing to talk, so I asked, "Why did you bring Mysir Moreau?"

She gave a heavy sigh and a shake of her head before responding. "Do you think you can meet my brother in public without a chaperone and there not be talk? My presence here, as well as Mysir Moreau's, makes it an acceptable party."

"So you did it to help me?"

I could tell she didn't like that suggestion.

"I did it to protect the Chambaux name," she said stiffly. "I knew he was a friend of yours and when I ran into him, and he was lamenting he had not seen tonight's play, I thought it an opportunity not to be missed. A couple implies romance, but a quartet is practically a party, making quite an acceptable number."

Tristan returned with Charlotte.

"I hear you've been causing trouble again," said my friend as she opened the door and scrambled inside.

"Nothing of the sort," I said, but was too tired to make it sound convincing.

Charlotte examined me as Tristan told her, "I thought it was simply a faint until I realized she had stopped breathing."

"How long did this last?" asked Charlotte, gently removing the fur from around my chest. Her fingers felt icy.

"Not long," said Valentina. "But it was very scary. Tristan insisted he could not hear her heart."

Charlotte took her listening tube, a stethoscope to my chest. "Breathe in deeply. Now again. Now cough." Then she took my wrist and counted my heartbeat, before using a sphygmograph to take my blood pressure.

Finished, she replaced my fur wrap and started putting her medical equipment back in the case. "You seem recovered from whatever happened, and I did not hear any abnormalities, but your heart rate is very low. You should get home, rest with some nice warm water bottles, and take some broth for breakfast with some weak tea. I'd add no excitement, but I don't give out advice that no one will take."

"You think her fine?" asked Tristan.

"She seems to be. But considering what you described as

happening, I would want her to get some rest. Go home, Elinor." She patted my hand and stepped back out. Standing outside, she added humorously, "I'll go examine the dead and send you all my notes. From what His Grace says it doesn't seem you'll be needing a Ghost Talker."

She said goodbye to us and headed back, stopped by Barbier on the way. Their heads close, they entered the Luminary together.

I felt a wave of disappointment. I wanted to see the bodies!

Tristan said sternly, "Doctor's orders, Elinor. You are going home to rest, even if I have to sit on you."

CHAPTER NINE

The next morning I awoke to a painful bruise on my chest and the feeling I had forgotten something. It took me a moment to realize what I had lost: Frida Korver.

Frida had sacrificed herself either to free or destroy the souls of the half-dead. I believed she had transitioned to the Afterlife, taking those poor creatures with her.

With her gone, I felt lighter, but also lost in melancholy. Tears rolled down my cheeks into my ears as I stared at the ceiling, contemplating the mystery of death.

I heard a masculine voice outside my door. Sitting up, I wiped my face with the back of my nightgown's sleeve. Taking my father's watch from where it lay on my bedside table, I opened the case and viewed the time. It was far too early for callers. Rolling out of bed, I slipped on my robe and cracked open the door.

Tristan Fontaine was sitting on my sofa eating a buttered roll while Anne-Marie poured him coffee. His tailored day suit, with creases ironed as sharp as a knife, did not suffer from the early hours of the morning. He propped his newspaper against the gleaming silver of the coffee pot and said, "Good morning, Elinor."

Pulling my robe tighter around me, I poked my head out further, saying, "Whatever are you doing here?"

"Making sure you're alive." To Anne-Marie, he commanded gently, "That will be all now."

She gave him a bobbing curtsy and, without even casting me a look, retreated to the kitchen. I was so outraged at her betrayal that I might have closed my bedroom door and sulked, but I was hungry and it was my home after all! Stalking over to a chair, I sat down, arms crossed.

Tristan slid me a cup of tea across the table. On the saucer was a lemon slice. He returned to his newspaper.

"No mention of the disturbance at the Luminary. I imagine de Windt told the reporters that any leaks about it would get them charged under the Crown's Subversive Disturbance Act. That's what I would have done." When I gave no response, he looked up and said, "I see you are still upset about me sending you home last night. Sometimes it's best to beat a retreat and fight another day. Would you have remained silent about how you removed the threat of those creatures?"

"Why do we need to keep de Windt in the dark?" I protested. "Wouldn't it be best to let him know what he faces?"

"Events at Hightower House are still recent in his mind. He is looking for something, anything, to drag us in for more questioning. Let Inspector Barbier and Dr. LaRue discuss these creatures and what their appearance means. We need to keep out of it unless you enjoy being behind bars. I certainly do not."

I reached over and started buttering a piece of toast.

"Why does he hate you so much?"

Tristan shrugged. "Hate? I think that's a strong word, but yes, well, he does seem to hold a vendetta. I am an easy target to blame for all that is wrong with His Majesty's decisions. Imagine if you actually took the man as he was— often petulant, capricious, and selfish. It would strain your loyalty if you saw him fall off the pedestal that people want to keep the royals on. So easier to dump your ire upon someone else. Someone who you think took a position you should have. And since you have aligned yourself with me, they lumped you into the same stew."

"You've worked so hard for the king. It seems very unfair."

"Perhaps." There was a long pause before he leaned forward, his arms resting on his thighs, his eyes concerned. "What I would prefer to talk about is what happened to you last night. You visited the Beyond, didn't you?"

I nodded. "The presence of so many dead-alive things drew out the souls that now reside within me. The girl souls that joined with me when I used them to destroy Parnell's Beyond palace and to sunder Vonn. They practically dragged me into the Beyond when those things showed up."

"Truly?" he asked, cocking his head. "Because I think you've been looking for an excuse ever since Madame Granger forbade that ghostly place."

"Now, Tristan, did I even try once to go into the Beyond when we were at Hightower?"

"Hm. No, but what I do remember is someone who tried to enter a graveyard after being warned by its dead guardian that to do so would be risky."

"He didn't say that. Exactly," I hedged.

"Elinor," he said warningly. "I was there. It is this reckless disregard for your own safety that we need to speak about."

I set aside what remained of my toast and clasped my hands tightly together in my lap. "Truly, I wouldn't have gone to the Beyond last night except that she drew me there. Frida Korver, she with the violin voice."

He shook his head. "You've lost me completely."

Over the rest of breakfast, I explained what had happened in the Beyond. How Frida had collected those damned souls and taken them with her, I hoped, to the Afterlife. At the end of my explanation, I said sadly, "I couldn't transition them, so she did. And now she is gone, I don't know where. Do you think you could find out who she was? I would like to speak with her family."

"I will try, but unfortunately, someone destroyed, or stole, all of Parnell's research documents. Unless her family is looking for her, it will be difficult, as her last name is very common."

"It's times like these that I am not sorry he is dead," I muttered to myself.

"Parnell isn't a ghost?" Tristan asked, curiously.

"I don't think so because I have not felt him about, but truthfully, I haven't looked. I have nothing to say to him, dead or alive." Squeezing the lemon into my tea, I asked, "Are you going to tell me what happened after you sent me home like a fretful child?"

"Right after you collapsed, the demonstration ended because all the protesters fell to the ground in a dead heap. It was as if they were puppets and someone had cut the strings. Of course, I figured you had something to do with that, hence your unconscious state. It was dramatic and inexplicable. Obviously your handiwork."

I bit my lip, trying to appear contrite. I don't think he bought it, as he only sighed and asked, "Now, do you want to know about Dr. LaRue's findings?"

"You could have begun with that!"

He forestalled me. "You'll want to read her notes in full at a later date. They are not to be digested along with breakfast, trust me. But I can give you a summary."

"Yes, please do! What did she discover?"

"As we thought, the protesters were of the same dead-alive persuasion of Lord Tremblay. They shoveled the remains into sacks. Not a job that the gendarmes really enjoyed, I'm afraid. One interesting thing the doctor discovered through her examination of teeth and bone was that they were the working class and had lived a hard life."

"Interesting. So a group of elderly poor people were given a life-suspending drug and sent to disrupt the theater? To accomplish what, exactly?" I pondered out loud.

"Do you not think those in age closer to death are easier to tempt with this new drug that promises an extension to your life? I believe they were sent to their deaths, hoping they would kill off the rest of us."

"How horrible. For them and us."

"Remember, you were worried about the gaslamps on stage? Your friend Moreau luckily got them shut off, for it turns out that the protesters' clothes were soaked with flammable oil. They would become human torches if any flame touched them."

The intensity of the precognitive vision from last night rushed over me, causing me to shudder. "How many would have died? We are dealing with someone truly evil."

Tristan's face was grim. "Our master criminal operates in the shadows and puts his pawns in harm's way. He does not care about human life if it gains him his objective."

"Which is what? I do not understand."

"Chaos. Disruption. The break-down of civil order."

We were both quiet. His words disturbed me so much that I set aside the muffin I had been covering with jam. "But the protesters at the Residency the other day were real people. They were normal enough."

"Last night I asked Barbier about that very thing. He detained a few of them for disorderly conduct. None of them exhibited any mad, erratic behavior. No, on the whole, they were a loud bunch who argued about the right to be held but otherwise were perfectly ordinary."

"So why was it different at the Luminary?"

Tristan leaned back on the sofa and sighed again. He was clearly disturbed and unhappy.

"Unfortunately, I think the answer lies in who attended the theater that night. It was the play to see. The sold-out show had seats filled with the cream of society. Valentina pointed some of them out— such as the ward of the king and Lady Talleyrand. I counted at least half a dozen from the House of Lords, a couple of judges, two well-known statesmen, and in the box opposite ours was His Majesty's latest mistress."

"Oh, I'm sorry I missed her! Was Lady Baudelaire sitting in her box?"

He ignored my question.

"Lady Talleyrand is in some delicate negotiations between the two houses of parliament, trying to get them to come together to calm down this unrest. If we were to lose her now-." He shook his head. "I'd hate to imagine it."

"How can one person have that much influence? Surely someone else could do it."

He shook his head. "Doubtful. She is a unique person. One of the few I respect. She can keep a level head even during the most acrimonious discussion, and both sides will listen to her. She is related to His Majesty, as most of the nobility is, but she can claim a closer connection than most, which endears her to Le beau idéal. For the common people, she has supported campaigns for better working conditions. Her charities are not just lip service, but actually provide real assistance to those in need. So destroying the Luminary last night and everyone in it would have exactly caused the disruption that I believe our master criminal wants."

My hand covered my mouth as a thought crossed my mind. "And you were there, Tristan. Do not forget that."

"I haven't. This morning, I have told Valentina to pack up and leave for Chambaux. She will be safest out of the city." He started toying with a teaspoon on the table as he added, his eyes not meeting mine. "I know you won't go, Elinor, but please consider it."

"To Chambaux? You must be joking! Isn't your mother there? I think I'll risk Alenbonné. It seems far safer."

"What about returning to Hightower?" he suggested.

"I think the Montaines have had enough of me, don't you think?"

The flat of his hand struck the table, making the cups shake in their saucers, and I jumped in place.

"Stop joking and take me seriously!"

"I am. I am. But I assure you, I'm not valuable at all."

"No? The woman who removed that entire threat at the theater while she was in a dead faint is not a risk to this criminal's plans?"

"That wasn't me. That was Frida Korver."

He bent forward, closing the distance between us, his irritation visible. "Stop this act of humility. The fact is, without you, Elinor, those in the theater would be dead. Do not discount your role in what happened, or didn't. Or that someone would want to stop you from interfering. Did you not tell me a few weeks ago that you thought someone was trying to kill you?"

"I'm staying here."

He sank against the sofa's back. Irritated still, but calmer. "I should have de Windt arrest you. That would keep you safe and sound. And I warn you, he would be happy to do it!"

"You wouldn't dare!"

He grimaced before sweeping a hand over his forehead, tousling his well-groomed head of hair. "I should. I really should. But you are right. I won't. Now, at least if you want to dash off following some clue, please notify me first. If you cannot reach me, you are to tell Stephan. Or the men I have set to guard you."

"It's really unnecessary to have these men following me about—"

His stern look made me stop talking.

"I will decide what is necessary for your safety, for you have no notion of taking any care. Now finish your breakfast like a good little girl and I will let you read Dr. LaRue's reports."

Charlotte's preliminary notes only confirmed what we all knew: the protesters at the Luminary were more dead than alive. There was not much that Tristan hadn't already told me. I handed them back.

"Do you think you could try to Ghost Talk their remains?"

"It would be a waste of time, for their flesh is too far dead to hold memory. Besides, I need eyes and tongue in order to get them to speak to me. Since Frida took their souls, they would not be ghosts either."

Tristan grimaced at my answer. "This summer, tension in the city has been rising especially around the docks, with the students, and in the poorer districts of the city. Malicious damage is on the rise to warehouses and the train lines. Threats have become very specific, not only to His Majesty but to key members in parliament."

I frowned. "I don't understand it. How does this serve our master criminal? How does it make him money?"

"They are playing for higher stakes than diamonds and gold, Elinor. The overthrow of the monarchy is their end game."

Before leaving Tristan pulled me into an embrace which was more chastising than romantic. "Now, Elinor, I know you don't want to talk about what happened last night. How you almost died, but you need to take some care right now."

"I didn't—"

He put his finger over my lips. "My sweet girl, you were one breath away from it. If you don't care about yourself, think about me. I was terrified."

"You were?" I said with wonder.

Holding my face with his hands, he gave me a deep kiss that fulfilled me like a flower receiving its first rain.

"Yes, I was. I think my hair will be white before the month is gone. So spare some thought to me and my health before you hare off to wreak havoc."

CHAPTER TEN

There is nothing like being told to stay in one place to make one want to rush about running errands. It took restraint to stay put. By the afternoon I was pacing the room, looking out the window, bored. It was lucky for my sanity that visitors arrived by afternoon tea to divert me.

Anne-Marie opened the door to a knock, and Twyla Andricksson entered with a quick step. Following her in a much slower manner was my old mentor, Leona Granger.

As she grabbed me in a rib-cracking hug, Twyla asked in that vibrant butterfly quick way, "Fetching earrings, Anne-Marie. Are those a gift from an admirer?"

Since I had last seen her in the spring, the girl had grown in height by a good inch, and her frame was leaving childhood behind and becoming that of a woman. I smiled. "It is good to see you, Twyla."

Holding my hands, she said, grinning, "Madame, you look so brown from the sun your freckles are showing! Anne-Marie says you were visiting the country. Where did you go? Was it a case? Did you see any ghosts?"

"Yes. I was visiting some friends of a friend. When did you return to town?"

"We came in on the train this morning, but Madame wanted to stop here first before we returned to the house."

As we talked, Leona slowly settled herself in a chair, while Anne-Marie hovered at her elbow in case she needed assistance. Leona seemed frailer than ever. The pale pink of her skin showed veins and bruises from age, and her tremble had grown so that when she placed her cane at her chair's side, it fell to the floor. Anne-Marie picked it up and placed it gently back into place.

"Dear child, how have you been?" she asked me.

Before I could answer, Twyla interrupted. "We did as much as we could for the mediums who had lost their way, and Madame Granger had to get back here to deal with the Society's business. Like always, they are causing another mess and she has to clean it up."

To Anne-Marie, I said, "Perhaps some refreshment after their long journey?" The young girl nodded and left to the kitchenette behind the green swing door.

Taking a seat on the couch opposite where Leona sat, I asked, "Are you still having problems because of what Parnell did?"

She shook her head, her white hair floating outward with its wisps like a cloud being pulled apart by the wind. "The girl exaggerates. It was the only time to come home and rest in my bed again. Besides, Twyla had done what she could."

Restless, Twyla wandered around the sitting room, touching the fresh roses arranged on the mantelpiece and running her finger along the rim of a blue and white porcelain bowl. She bent over to closely examine a pair of silver candlesticks, before examining a watercolor on the wall.

I congratulated my former apprentice. "And what good work it's been! Three mediums brought back to being themselves."

"I should say so! No one else could have done it."

The girl was not one to be shy about her accomplishments and thus did not pretend any humility. Some might call her brash, but considering her abilities, you could say she was only being truthful.

Leona tapped her palm on her armchair. "Child, tame your arrogance!"

Twyla shot Leona a glare from flashing green eyes before quickly lowering her lashes. In a meek tone, quite unfamiliar to the girl I had known, she replied, "You're right, Madame Granger."

I tried to lighten the mood by being cheerful. "Well, it is good to have you both back. Now Twyla can finish her apprenticeship with me."

Leona quickly contradicted that suggestion. "You are mistaken, Elinor. Twyla will not be under your guidance. She needs a firmer hand than you can give her."

This king of barbed remark, couched with mild politeness, was what Leona specialized in giving. Politeness meant you could not directly address the remark and if you did, she would only state you were being too sensitive and had taken her meaning out of context. I loved her, but I was also honest about her faults.

However, Twyla had no such restraint and protested. "Madame Chalamet was an excellent mentor! I learned so much from her in the short time I was with her."

"Thank you for defending me, Twyla," I said, giving her a smile to know how much I appreciated her support. "However, I was unaware of your unique talent of being able to travel the Beyond at will, so perhaps I wasn't the best teacher after all."

"My Morpheus teachers didn't know either. I would have brought it up if I had known it was anything unusual," the girl said.

"How was your trip to the country, Elinor?" Leona asked, firmly changing the subject. She always did this, ignoring the things she didn't want to address.

"Restful," I lied.

Before leaving town, she had strongly advised me not to do any work involving ghosts, an order which I had disobeyed. She didn't need to know that I was now carrying three souls from the girls Parnell Lafayette had murdered in his obscene quest for knowledge about the Beyond. Or that I had let a young woman escape justice by blaming a dead man for the murder she had committed. She had her secrets, as I did.

"I feel fully recovered and ready to get back to work."

She looked doubtful. "Do you think that is wise? I was just telling Twyla on the train journey back that perhaps it was time for you to think of retirement. Or taking a leave of absence."

If Leona was determined to deliver unpleasant surprises, she was certainly very good at it today. She was reminding me why over the last few years I had visited her less and less.

I attempted to sound lighthearted. "Retire? That is probably best applied to you, madame, then myself."

She continued on her theme. Nothing could stop her when she had something to say, especially if it was one of her lectures about what she thought you should do. "You have your entire life ahead of you. It's about time you gave up this quest for revenge. Trying to find your father's murderer has gotten you nowhere and wasted the best years of your life."

"I assure you, I do not feel it has been a waste."

"But have you discovered any news? None. It is time to look at a new beginning before you get too old to have one. Twyla informs me that there is someone in your life now, though the naughty girl refused to give me a name. Best to get married and start a family before it's too late."

At this point Twyla knocked over a small box from a side table. With a grimace, she held it up to show that one broken hinge had caused the lid to close crookedly.

Her clumsiness helped cool my rising anger. I didn't want to get into an argument with my former mentor. She was old and had her ways; they just weren't my ways.

"Take that into the kitchen. Anne-Marie has a shelf where she puts things that need repairing." Twyla practically ran off to do as I bade.

"Awkward child," clucked Leona disdainfully. "If it wasn't for her brilliant talent, I swear I could not stand the girl for one more moment. In the last month alone, she put shoe blacking on my best hat and ripped the hems of too many skirts to count."

Thinking back to my time with Twyla, I couldn't help but reluctantly agree that the girl could be a challenge. However, Leona was being too harsh, probably because it had been some time since she had been so young. "She grows on you, though. She is quite sincere, with no maliciousness in her."

"Perhaps. But she needs to be taught with a firm hand, Elinor, and that is why she will be staying with me. Her talent could become very destructive, not only to herself, but to others." It made me wonder what had happened since Twyla had left, but it was clear my old mentor was not going to reveal more.

Leona liked to cultivate an aura of mystery and wisdom that had made her career as a Ghost Talker very lucrative. Under that absentminded, wispy facade, she was also crafty, and this served her well in managing the Morpheus Society members. Any members who might wish to cross her found out too late, she wasn't as dreamy-minded as they had thought. It was hard to hold water in your hands. Or grab smoke.

Her next words brought me out of my reverie.

"I'm serious. I want you to give some thought to stepping back from Ghost Talking. You only got into it because of your father's death, not because of any genuine interest in the subject itself. You were never one of the talented ones. Not at all like Twyla."

I was finding this entire conversation unpleasant. Whereas before, I had always excused Leona's belittlements of my achieve-ments, putting it down to her desire to keep her ascendancy as my teacher. *She is old, set in her ways*, I reminded myself.

"Thank you for your concern, Leona. While I may have started my work with ghosts because of my father's foul murder, I do believe I have found a vocation in helping others dealing with their grief."

She gave me a look filled with pity. "My dear girl, I'm sorry to tell you, but you may not have an option. There have been complaints."

"Complaints?" I replied, surprised. "About me?"

"Yes."

"I didn't receive any formal paperwork about this. Who is complaining? About what, exactly?"

"Nothing official. As of yet. The Society's reputation took several blows when news of Parnell's seduction of those girls became public. We cannot withstand any more mud slung upon our reputation. Expulsion from the Society will result from any misconduct to serve as an example."

We were back to Society politics and what had produced Parnell. Like Tristan, I was being attacked from within by my own organization. "Who is complaining about me? What are they saying?"

She waved a hand covered in black lace at me. "Do not think I believe them worthy. I only came here to warn you. So far, they are only insinuations. Gossip."

"Insinuations? Exactly what does this gossip accuse me of?"

Her mouth puckered like she had tasted a lemon. Sighing, she told me, "Trickery, Elinor, if you must know. That you are faking messages from the Beyond for money. I hope it is not true, but I know your love for a stage magician's tricks. How enthralled you were by the card tricks and the rabbit in the hat when the circus was in town. Can you really say you've never used such tricks?"

My mind immediately swept through all the interactions I had had with clients over the last year. Had I used tricks? Sometimes. Like the falling coins at Lindengaard during the Winter Revels. Embellished messages? Perhaps with Jakobsen, the merchant whose business partner had died. I had ordered him to do good by imitating the dead man's voice.

But I never outright faked messages that harmed my clients. I seldom charged clients the amounts other mediums did. Some I didn't charge at all.

Leona reached out to pat my hand. "My child, I do not blame you. We all exaggerate a bit of our talents. After all, would they really believe if we didn't add a bit of drama to our performance? There is no shame in that, but if they brought you to court on fraud charges? Well, I fear no one except myself would come forth to defend you."

"Does this have to do with Parnell's friends still in the Society?"

"It is true he had a following in our numbers, and that some of them are very displeased with your involvement in the matter. They wanted his immortality research to continue, you see. Especially those of our more senior members who have influence."

"Like yourself?"

She gave a raspy chuckle. "I'm far too gone, my girl, to benefit from some sort of immortality in the Beyond. When my spirit is free from this creaky old body, I will not be sorry."

Feeling a rush of sympathy toward her, I was almost rash enough to tell her that Parnell's research was being used to extend an unnatural life to the dying. However, at that moment, Twyla returned.

At the appearance of her protégé, Leona used her cane to prop herself to standing. "I do believe we need to get on with our day as it is late and I fear we are keeping you from your supper. Think about what I said. It might be wise to take a break until things calm down. These things often stem from jealousy and will burn themselves out if you provide no more fuel than they can use. Such happened to me once, but I was patient and the rumors dropped away. Twyla, say your goodbyes."

I walked with them down to the hotel foyer, and then to the street. Leona's conversations were trivialities about the weather and the train ride back. Twyla asked about ghosts I was working with, and if I had any more killers following me around. She was a bit disappointed when I said no. Perhaps when we had time to be private, I would tell her about the Gray Lady's warning and Lord Tremblay's strange ending.

After waving them off, I returned to my rooms. Anne-Marie was plumping the sofa pillows but upon seeing me, she stopped and fished out a folded piece of paper from her apron pocket. "Twyla wanted me to give this to you."

"Twyla?" Unfolding it, I read silently: *We must meet without Mme. Granger knowing. It is about your father.*

Stunned, I heard Anne-Marie say far away, "It was good seeing Twyla again, but did she not seem too quiet?"

"Leona is trying to tame her, Anne-Marie," I said absentmindedly, still trying to understand the girl's note. Frowning, I asked, "Did she say anything to you that seemed unusual when you were in the kitchen?"

Anne-Marie said, "No. Only that I was to give you that after she left."

"She is staying at Madame Granger's town house, is she not?"

"That was my understanding," said Anne-Marie. "Is something wrong?"

"No. I only wanted to know how to reach her. We must find Marcus. I shall need him."

CHAPTER ELEVEN

I t was a week later that a curious chance meeting resulted in me running to escape arrest.

Since seeing Twyla and receiving her mysterious message I had tried twice to see her. Once I was told she was indisposed. The second time, no one was at home. Blocked, I put Marcus on the problem. He was to watch and arrange a way to communicate with my apprentice, for such I still considered her.

Charlotte checked on me but found me disgustingly healthy (her words).

"You sound almost disappointed!" I exclaimed as I re-buttoned my blouse.

"Not disappointed, but I don't like anomalies and you are one." She re-buckled her medical case, preparing to leave.

"Have you heard any more from Dr. Devereaux? About his patient, who fears death?"

"Armand is still trying to get the man to agree to see you. I now wish I hadn't bothered bringing it to your attention. His patient is probably a professional time-waster. One of these individuals who seek attention by exaggerating their symptoms in order to gain sympathy. They latch onto anyone who shows them the slightest interest."

"Are you accusing me of faking my symptoms?" I asked her, laughing.

She jerked, surprised. "Sorry. I didn't mean you. It's only that I've seen these types before. Always a new mysterious pain that nothing seems to cure. They show up every week, asking for another pill or potion, complaining again about something else. Time-wasters," she repeated dismissively.

"I don't know," I said doubtfully. "Dr. Devereaux's patient seemed to have a very specific fear, and I would like to see this talk cure in action. Maybe he will change his mind and agree to see me. I hope so."

"Maybe," said Charlotte in a tone that said she did not think he would.

Tristan I only saw once, but he sent notes and flowers when he could not come. I could not prevent myself from feeling that perhaps he was avoiding me because of my refusal to his proposal. The thought put me in very low spirits.

Cleared by my doctor, I decided it was time to return to my regular duties. The list that Twyla had made long ago of my cabinet of herbs and medicinals showed several things I had still to re-stock. Intending to stay busy and not think of a certain duke, I paid a visit to my local chemist only to find that the few items I wanted were all out of stock.

"Sorry, madame, but I haven't gotten a shipment in for at least two months. It's probably sitting at some dock warehouse waiting for an inspector to stamp it," said the chemist, standing behind her dispensing counter.

"I don't understand why that would hold things up," I responded, slightly irritated at being disappointed.

"It's the new taxes. Everything coming in from Perrino must have the stamp on it indicating the import taxes were paid, you see," she explained. "Nothing I can do about it."

"Hm. Well, when do you think it will be here?"

"Next month? Hard to say."

"Fine. I'll check by then, shall I?"

"You do that, madame."

My irritation is the only reason I can claim being distracted on my return to the Crown. I cut through the large park where once I had met Parnell Lafayette to retrieve a baron's missing daughter. This shortcut would bring me to another, busier street where I would be sure to find a quick-cab.

Passing through, I found a large crowd congregating around one of the park fountains. Curious, I came closer, but being short, could not see what everyone was looking at.

"Excuse me," I said, worming my way through the press until I gained a spot at the front where I could see what had attracted their attention. On the rim of the concrete basin of the fountain stood a young man in his twenties, who was shouting.

The speaker wore the casual wear of the student, meaning a bit too garish with its informal day coat of bottle green, and the trousers in tan with the red plaid line. His dark brown hair was tied back and his mustache elegantly waxed. He was holding his hat in his right hand and using it to emphasize his words.

"Your neck is under the boot of these nobles. They control the food we eat, when we eat, and how much. Is your child hungry tonight? I know I'm hungry! Hungry for being treated as equal. Hungry to sit at the head of the table."

Tables? Food? What was this all about?

"We are men. We have rights. Rights that are ours upon our birth. Not to be given to us by our so-called betters!"

Oh, he was one of them. One of those rabble-rousers that Barbier thought little of.

An arm being raised by the person next to me knocked my

shoulder and I moved sideways to avoid another encounter. It put me next to someone new. Someone I recognized. Theodoor Vischeer, the botanist I had met at Lindengaard during the Winter Revels and who had been at the Luminary with Lady Tulip.

"Mysir Vischeer," I greeted him.

"Madame Chalamet," he said, in a pleased manner. "How good of you to come to our little meeting." Thoroughly modern, he shook my hand as if I were a man instead of giving it the slight squeeze that was the traditional greeting between the sexes. "Are you enjoying the speech? Olivier is doing quite well, I think."

I turned my attention back to the orator.

"They have harnessed us like beasts and we have plowed their fields, only to be shut away in the stables. Is it not time that we insist on being treated like men instead of oxen?"

"He does seem to have a powerful turn of phrase," I said diplomatically.

Vischeer grinned. "He does indeed."

"Is he a friend of yours?"

"In a manner of speaking, yes." Vischeer looked over my head as if something had suddenly alerted him. I had the impression of a fox scenting the breeze, catching a warning whiff of the hunter's dog. "However, I think it is time we beat a diplomatic retreat."

He made a strange gesture to someone across from us, who nodded back. With a hand on my elbow, he guided me around the front of the crowd, circling the fountain until we were behind Olivier.

"I'm afraid that this get-together is going to be gate-crashed by some unwelcome guests. It's best we get ahead of the storm."

I craned my neck and saw the blue caps pushing their way through the crowd. Two short blasts of a whistle sounded and I heard a shout for the crowd to disperse.

"Come along," Vischeer said calmly as chaos broke out around us.

A rock flew by my head to hit someone else who yelped,

clutching their head. Dragged along by Vischeer who had increased his pace, I would have stumbled except that a large hand under my other elbow steadied me.

A familiar voice told me, "Be careful, madame." It was Farrow. The man Tristan had set to guard me.

I was lucky to have them both because otherwise I would quickly have been trampled in the mayhem. The crowd was trying to separate, splinter and run, but the gendarmes were pushing at three of the four sides, trying to force us into one direction. I didn't think that was a good idea, and neither did Vischeer.

"No," he said, resisting the forward propulsion created by those around us as he dragged me sideways. "We need to go this way."

Farrow was swiveling his head in an attempt to keep a view of everything at once. I grabbed his sleeve and tugged to get his attention. "Can you make a way for us?"

Farrow's bulk pushed through, and we found ourselves on the edge of the mob. At that moment, someone else got into a grapple with an officer who shouted for assistance. Three other gendarmes came to his aid, giving us a chance to break away and flee from the group being rounded up by the gendarmes.

Vischeer grabbed my wrist, dragging me into a run, forcing me to pick up my skirt to prevent being hobbled. I could hear Farrow following behind, breathing hard like a freight train. We crossed the street and entered an alley. Vischeer did not stop, so neither did we. Running down the narrow way made me think unpleasantly of my misadventure with Vonn in the Beyond. Thankfully, it was quickly over and we emerged onto another street.

Everything here was calm and normal. Vischeer slowed to a walk, letting go of my hand to remove his hat and to smooth his hair before replacing it on his head.

"Thanks for the assistance... ?" he said to Farrow, who notably did not supply his name in return.

Instead, to me, he said, "I think it best we return to the Crown, madame."

"After we just renewed our acquaintance?" said Vischeer, showing a bit of humor. His nonchalant manner after what had just happened made me wonder if he made it a habit of running from the gendarmes. "There is a matter I actually wish to discuss with you, Madame Chalamet. Perhaps we could talk over a cup?"

Farrow's disapproval of this plan was clear, but I ignored him. "Do you think your friend Olivier is all right?"

"Oh, the Brotherhood will have gotten him out of that pickle. He'll find a hole to go aground and be back at the game by tomorrow."

"You know him well?"

"He's working on his upper levels. A historian. Be careful with those types. They see the future by looking at the past." He tapped his temple.

All of this time we had been walking down what seemed to be the quietest of streets, life as normal as can be. It was unsettling to know that a block or two over people were being chased down by the gendarmes, about to be arrested, and that I could have been one of them.

Perhaps sitting down for a brief rest would be best. A good cup of tea would not be amiss. Besides, I was curious about what Vischeer wanted to discuss.

"Do you know, I think I'll take you up on your offer. Once I have a moment to regain myself, we can catch a quick-cab and go home."

My protector grimaced but did not protest. After all, he was not in charge of me, only of my protection.

"Good. Right around this corner, there's a diner."

The diner was a long narrow wooden shack where you could sit up against an exterior counter that ran the length of the building. It was a place where worker between shifts could grab a quick meal before going home or returning to work.

I had never been to such a place. Feeling adventurous, I perched on a stool, my feet dangling. Farrow did not join us, preferring to stand at the corner, leaning against a post looking like an idler.

"What would you like?" Vischeer asked, pointing at a menu chalked on a board that hung beside a square window. From it issued a powerful smell of fried onion.

I hesitated. "What would you recommend?"

"A beer and a meat pastry?"

"Yes."

It was hours past the time of a usual daytime meal, so there was no line. He came back carrying two mugs.

"Have you been able to continue your botanical studies since I saw you at the Winter Revels, Mysir Vischeer?"

"I did. Although I also teach and tutor. My family has a noble lineage, but that doesn't bring in the royals, and I find I like to eat."

Though his coat lacked the glove-fitting tailoring of Tristan's outfits, its quality was better than what Inspector Barbier wore. But he had no man servant for his shoes were not shined, nor was there a darning of where probably ash from a pipe had left a little hole in one sleeve. Vischeer wore no jewelry, and his cuff links were of plain pewter. The only real sign of any influence was the watch chain that seemed of gold-plated brass, but I would need to touch it to know for sure.

Yes, he was a man who seemed to have one foot in each world.

"You may have already heard, but the university has closed all classes until this unrest resolves." He took a contemplative sip of his beer.

"My friend, Dr. LaRue, whom you met at Lindengaard, also has suspended her teaching lectures. At the Luminary the other evening, I noticed that you were with Lady Langenberg."

The mention of Tulip's name made the tips of his ears grow slightly pink, although his face gave nothing away. Since saving the girl from the horrible attentions of Lord Jansen Buckard, I had heard little from her. Considering the differences in our class and the circumstances of our meeting, that did not surprise me.

"Yes. The Luminary." He stopped, his eyelids fluttering as he thought. "That was a horrible night. We did see you while we were evacuating. It was later, when we had time to discuss what happened, that she urged me to contact you. She told me I could trust you to keep what I told you confidential."

His comment made me think of Valentina's recent problem with the king's letters and how I had already broken my promise by telling Tristan about them. "I try to be discreet, but sometimes I can't guarantee it. For example, if I feel withholding information from others would be dangerous, I may not keep your confidence."

He gave me a very nice smile. "I think if you had promised absolute discretion, I would not have believed you. And yes, I do think the information is dangerous, but I do not know who to share it with. Or if anyone would believe me, it sounds so fantastic."

Really, it was up to him if he wanted to take the risk. I did not push him.

At that moment, his name was called, and he went back to the window to collect our order. He returned with two paper packets and handed one to me. Instead of eating his food, he laid it aside with a sigh.

"What I'm about to say sounds unbelievable, but what if I told you that there are things walking around, appearing to be like you and me, but are really nothing but a warm corpse? That those at the Luminary were such?"

"I know they were."

"Then you know about these creatures?" His face was relieved.

"Yes, they were at the Luminary that night. Now, tell me what you think others won't believe that you feel has bearing upon this matter."

He began his tale.

CHAPTER TWELVE

W hat *Theodoor Vischeer told me:*
With the civil unrest, some students have returned home to families or taken work outside of Alenbonné. Others decided to take the Perino grand tour and see some of their famous art collections.

Still, a few stay. Waiting to see what happens. Hoping they can make things better. For Alenbonné is our home and we shall not desert her in her hour of need.

While classes are not being held, I have taken to tutoring advanced students who desire to use this time to improve their knowledge of the natural world. Also, the plants in the greenhouse have daily needs, no matter what is happening with humanity.

This means I am still working in the student quarter. The curfew and the guardia patrols have made us all cautious. They need little provocation to treat us like common criminals.

For this reason I pay attention to those in public areas more than I normally would. Who belongs and who does not, and especially when they behave oddly.

So when I saw half a dozen people walking down the middle of the street, it caught my attention immediately. While others locked their doors and closed their shutters, I was curious what they were about, so I ducked into a doorway to watch them pass me by.

Considering the circumstances, perhaps it was foolish, but I decided to follow them. It was their bizarre behavior that intrigued me. While the rest of us were being careful and creeping about like mice, they were parading about, shouting violence and waving sticks over their heads.

I call them a group, but they barely acted as a cohesive whole. None of them spoke to each other. Each one acted as if they were alone, shouting some garbled nonsense I could not decipher. The sticks they waved over their heads were old lumber, probably salvaged from one of the derelict buildings that are common in the student quarter.

They seemed to have no plan, no goal, as they randomly swung their clubs about. While they broke shop windows, they did no plundering and only continued down the street, leaving a path of destruction behind them.

As I followed them, dodging into doorways and hiding behind corners, I noticed something else. They seemed to have a leader— or at least a man who was more intelligent than the others. Whenever anyone lagged or strayed from the group, he cuffed and cursed them, forcing them back into some formation.

He was a big man, with a round face and short pudgy hands, and moved like a sack of laundry.

But his outfit alarmed me the most. His trousers were navy blue with the red trim down the leg, as all the guardia uniforms have. But while his coat matched in color, the braid was missing, as well as any identification badges on it. I believed this to be some underhanded attempt by the gendarmes to cause trouble in our quarter. I could see us being blamed for this violence and it providing an excuse for more arrests or searches of our homes.

However, before I could turn away, something startling happened that made me rethink all of my suppositions.

One of their number collapsed on the street. The group

walked on, ignoring him. When their leader came over to examine him, he kicked the poor misfortunate once or twice. The prone man did not rise, and his abuser muttered a string of curses before leaving him as he was.

The group made their way down the street and when they were out of sight; I thought of helping the fallen man. Perhaps he could tell me what was going on, so I crossed the street and went to check on the poor soul.

Vischeer visibly shuddered, closing his eyes briefly.

Imagine my horror when I discovered the heap was not a living being at all! It was only a sack of deflated skin, boneless, like a spent pig's bladder, its eyes now only hollow sockets.

It was the most terrifying thing I've ever seen in my life.

I must admit to my shame that I left it as it was, and spent the week trying not to think of it, or when I did, telling myself that it was only my imagination.

However, that night in the Luminary made me realize that what I experienced was real. Tulip and I were both trapped in our row of seats as the protesters were blocking either end. I climbed over our seats and helped her over and in this way, we made our way to the back of the exit.

Before we made it, there was an unholy shrieking whine that pierced the air like the sound of a wet log in a hot fire. I saw the protesters fall as one to the floor as a tremendous smell arose in the closed air.

I stopped Tulip from looking, but I knew what they were. They were the same thing as the body I had found in the street in the student quarter several weeks before.

At the end of his tale, Mysir Vischeer said, "You see why I have told no one. Who would believe that?"

"I would," I replied. "Now, tell me more of the group in the student quarter. Did you find out any more about them? Where they came from? Where they went?"

"I'm afraid I wanted nothing more than to forget the incident. And who was I to report it to? The gendarmes? With the unrest, to be connected to anything unusual would mean hours of interrogation by the gendarmes and likely a jail cell. Nowadays, they will arrest a man simply for walking down the street."

"Do you still think the gendarmes sent them to cause trouble?"

"The only thing that makes any sense to me is that King Guénard is doing this to make it easier to arrest us. When I later told Lady Tulip about the incident and its connection to events at the Luminary, she urged me to confide in you. She said that you were the person to understand anything supernatural."

I smiled. "She was right to do so, for I have knowledge of matters that concern the dead. What you found in the street was human, but late to its grave." I set aside my meat pie and its greasy newsprint wrapper on the counter. The fatty contents had made my stomach squirm, especially when you added Vischeer's tale to the meal. "What you have confided to me is indeed worrisome."

"Worrisome, madame? I call it terrifying. What are they? Where did they come from? What do they want?"

"I only know a few answers to your many questions. They are people just like us. Not monsters. Desperate people who, due to illness, used a drug to preserve their life. Unfortunately, when the drug runs its course, the body collapses into the state it would have attained if death had run its natural course."

He didn't look happy to hear my thoughts on the matter and asked impatiently, "Who is supplying this drug? Where does it come from?"

"That is the conundrum. The original creator is no longer of this earth, and his research has been stolen by person or persons unknown."

"But this leader of the mob? When I described him, you were about to say something and then stopped."

"There is a Sergeant Dupont who has gone missing from the force. Maybe it is him? But I would need to see him myself to confirm."

We both lapsed into silence. It was as if Farrow sensed we had come to the end of our conversation, for he turned my way and gave me a jerk of his head, trying to urge me to leave. Yes, it was starting to get late, but no. There was something we needed to discuss further.

"You mentioned that your friend Olivier was a member of the Brotherhood. What did you mean by that?"

Vischeer who had been staring at his beer in contemplation, gave me a sideways glance. "I shouldn't have mentioned that."

"But you did."

He twisted around on his stool, crossing his arms to stare at me. "Do you think it is fair that the house of Lords gets sixty-four members to the Commons thirty-eight?"

"Truthfully, I've never thought about it. What they do in Parliament has little to do with ghost talking. One is mundane, the other is spiritual."

"So if it doesn't apply to you, it's of no importance?" he demanded sharply. "Let me speak of something that would concern you as a woman. The divorce courts only let the man initiate the proceedings, not the woman. Women must list a man as guardian in order to hold property or a bank account. While the House of Lords has women members, they must have a title and be married. And these members cannot vote, only attend and speak."

"But what of Lady Talleyrand? I have heard that she wields quite a bit of power in government halls."

"She does. But that is through the force of her personality and her relation to the king. While I admire her, it still doesn't fix the problem that the Commons has no female members. Do you think that is right? As a working woman surely you want representation or do you think your sex is too frail and intellectually weak to serve in that capacity?"

"Of course not."

Vischeer was correct that I had given it little thought. Politics seemed to have nothing to do with how I lived with my life. Since most of my clientèle had been the middle and working class or the dead in the city morgue, I had ignored the social chasms between the classes. I did not bank, but used cash. My father's old workshop was in trust to me, with financial representatives being my guardians. At my death, any estate I had gained would go to my descendant if male; if female, it would be under a trust. If I had no issue at my death, the state would take it.

None of this had mattered to me. Until Tristan.

Farrow pulled out his pocket watch and made an elaborate show of checking the face before glaring my way. I ignored him.

"Representation is all we are asking," said Vischeer.

"How would women play a part in making that happen? We cannot vote. Who would fill these seats of yours, if given?"

"It would need men to step forward to advocate for our sisters and mothers."

"Someone like the Brotherhood?" His eyes held a gleam, but he said neither yea nor nay to my question. Thinking of Lady Tulip, I changed tactics. "Why is this your battle? I thought you were noble?"

"My mother is. My father isn't. But don't think the Groendyke family is like the Chambaux line. We have a small estate with a leaking roof, and I paid for my education by assisting my professors until I could teach. But forget about me. This is about Sarnesse. What we could be as a country versus what we are."

"From your friend Olivier's speech, are you advocating to gain this through violence?"

"No. I *prefer*," he stressed the last word, "that we work together, high and low, to bring about what is best for all citizens. A revolt is not an option I would wish for my country."

"Revolt!" I exclaimed, taken aback by the word. "Is that what your Brotherhood plans to do? If so, they will meet hard resistance from the King's men."

He gave me an intent stare. "It is not my desire for this to happen, understand me, but there are certain members who are trying to move us toward that end. The problem is that those who are advocating violence are subtle in their argument and have been winning people over to their idea."

"How can I help you prevent that from happening?" I asked, thinking he already had a scheme.

"Perhaps a friend of the Duke de Archambeau could be told my fears? And he might arrange a meeting? Unofficially, of course."

"Unofficially, I can do that," I agreed. "But I cannot guarantee what he would do with that information."

Vischeer said sternly, "If he tries to go against us, he will find escalation will do him no good. No, the only way this can end is if King Guénard agrees to our request to increase the seats in the Commons. That would calm down my comrades for now, but it must be soon. People without bread on the table cannot hold on to their reason for long."

"I shall tell him. How can I reach you?"

He pulled out a card from an inner pocket of his coat and scribbled an address on the back with a stubby pencil. "Here. Someone will get word to me. Now, I think your guardian is about to march over here and punch my nose, so probably it is best that we part. Good evening, Madame Chalamet."

CHAPTER THIRTEEN

The next morning, Charlotte met me at breakfast to tell me that the man who feared death was ready to meet me.

"Quiet as the grave around here," she said, taking the chair next to mine in the dining room of the Crown.

"Hm," I responded, my thoughts elsewhere. Twyla. Vischeer, Tristan, and not necessarily in that order. Last night I had sent a note to Tristan requesting a meeting but had yet to hear from him.

The Crown's head server immediately came over to see if we needed anything more.

"Just coffee, Pierre," Charlotte told him. After he left, she leaned forward and said again, "Quiet as a grave. Seems things are as unsettled here as they are through the city."

"Most of the visitors have left Alenbonné, and there are only a handful of long-term residents, like myself, who keep rooms here," I told her.

"It's the heat. And the humidity. Everyone hates the humidity the last few weeks in summer," she said, nodding her head sagely.

"I think it's more than that."

The coffee pot arrived, and Pierre poured it out before returning to stand at the end of the hotel's empty dining room.

There was no cheerful chatter, clinking of plates and silverware. Charlotte was right that the place was unnaturally quiet.

"Do you remember Msyir Vischeer? We met him at the Winter Revels. The botanist."

Charlotte looked up at the ceiling in thought. "Oh yes, I remember him now. Seemed to be interested in that flower girl you saved from a 'fate worse than death' as the scandal sheets like to phrase it."

"Lady Tulip Langenberg," I agreed.

"What about him?" She took a sip of coffee. Making a satisfied face, she raised her cup in a salute to Pierre, who had the good training only to return her a small smile. "Good coffee can bring you back from the dead."

"I ran into him yesterday evening in the park and he told me some disturbing things." Charlotte gestured with her cup for me to keep going. "He's seen a group of these people in the university quarter and, from the description of their leader, I think it was Sergeant Dupont."

"Dupont?" Charlotte exclaimed. "That doesn't sound like what he would do."

"What do you know about him?"

"Not much. Not a talkative man. A boring block of wood is how I'd describe him. They transferred him to work under Barbier a few years back. Why do you think it is him?"

"He's gone missing, and the physical description fits. Dupont has left the force without explanation."

"Do you think he's another one of the Ghastlys?" At my puzzled frown she expounded, "That's what I'm calling these creatures. If you had to examine what was left of them you'd understand why."

"Ah. Well, I'm not sure. He was acting with more intelligence than the others. But so did Lord Tremblay at Hightower. That is until he stopped taking Lafayette's drug mixture. Have you heard anything about this?"

Charlotte shook her head. "But then again, classes aren't being held, so I'm not seeing students on a regular basis. And my hours aren't the same as others since I am often in the morgue whenever I'm needed. I guess I thought the shops being closed was only happening around the university due to the friction between the gendarmes and the residents."

I sighed. There were two people I trusted without reservation: Charlotte and Tristan. I needed to tell someone, and he wasn't here, curse him. "He told me there was an underground political group called the Brotherhood."

"Oh. I've heard about them," said Charlotte in a tone that meant she didn't think much of what she knew. "Attended one of their lectures. Want to change the world. Idealists. There's always some of those at the university until they have to earn a living and life knocks it right out of them. Eating is far more useful than lofty dreams."

I wiped my mouth with my napkin and laid it beside my plate.

"From what he hinted, I fear that they are plotting something more dire than protests and throwing rocks at store windows."

Charlotte scratched her temple. "What more could they do? That seems enough to me."

"Violence against the Crown itself."

"I'm assuming you don't mean this hotel?" Charlotte said with a hint of wry humor.

"I do not."

"Have you told His Grace about this?"

"I've sent him a message. I haven't heard from him yet."

"Hm. If I hear anything more about this Brotherhood, I'll send a message to you. I do have a few living clients, such as my landlady and the greengrocer. A few in the neighborhood might know more than I. I'll ask about."

"Thank you, Charlotte." I sighed again and let the tension go out of my shoulders. "Now, what about Dr. Devereaux and his client, who fears being buried alive? Why did he agree to meet me?"

"Like I told you, the man is a time-waster, and Armand is probably tired of it. He gave him an ultimatum: meet you or get out."

"Oh, I don't want to see him if he doesn't really want to."

Charlotte rolled her eyes. "Some of these types you have to give a swift kick up the backside. I wouldn't lose any sleep over it."

We left with plenty of time to make our appointment. With the uncertainty of catching a quick-cab and the possibility of road-blocks I didn't want to risk arriving late. I had commissioned a carriage, which cost me a bit more, but had room enough for three.

"Who is this?" asked Charlotte as I waved Farrow over from where he had been sitting in the Crown lobby, pretending to read a newspaper.

"My bodyguard. Courtesy of His Grace." When Farrow joined us, I explained the situation to him. "I am going to a meeting and didn't think you would easily find another cab to follow us, so it's probably for the best if you just come with us."

He looked uncomfortable with this plan. His eyes going back and forth between me and Charlotte. "I'm usually more effective if no one knows about me."

"I understand, but this will be easier on everyone."

We arrived on time to discover the man we were to meet was already dead.

Dr. Armand Devereaux had a modest resident in Bonecutter's Alley. Originally, butchers and barbers had plied their trade here, but a fire caused much of Alenbonné to be rebuilt decades ago. In its place were these fine rows of houses that served as offices and residents of doctors who cured both physical and mental ailments.

Unlike Parnell's address in the same district, Dr. Devereaux's office held a more elite position, being nearer the park. His building exterior was white with black shutters, and the door had small topiary evergreen trees on either side of the step.

We knocked, and I heard a sound of rushing feet inside right before Dr. Devereaux opened the door. The look of crushing disappointment on his face might have made me laugh, except for the seriousness of his greeting.

He was in a state of excited worry, with a flushed face. "Oh, Madame! Charlotte! Dr. LaRue! I was expecting the gendarmes. He's dead!" We stood for a moment facing each other before he added hastily, "Come in. Come in."

Farrow couldn't have cared less about the dead patient. He faded away, drifting around the corner, presumably to make himself invisible. Charlotte and I entered the foyer, and Dr. Devereaux quickly shut the front door behind us.

"Do you mean Mysir Boutin?" I asked.

"Yes," he returned. Striding toward the base of the staircase, and mounted the steps, urging us to follow. "I found him dead in his bed less than a quarter of an hour ago."

"Any signs of violence?" asked Charlotte, whose mind always veered to a criminal explanation.

"Not that I can tell, but I'll let you be the judge. You have far more experience with that than I."

We traveled down a short hall before we entered a bedroom where the door was ajar. It was a safe assumption that the body lying under the sheet was that of Mysir Forrest Boutin's.

To one side of the bed went Charlotte, and I the other. She picked up a small mirror from the nightstand and held it up to the man's blue-lipped mouth. It did not fog.

"Was it you who closed his eyes?" she asked Devereaux.

"Yes. No pulse. No reaction to a pin-prick either."

I bent over and examined the face closely. He was a fleshy man and in repose, the skin on his face had folded down, causing deep crevices around his nose and mouth. The neck muscles had loosened and made his double chin appear thicker than it probably would have been if animated by life.

While Charlotte examined the body, I questioned Dr. Devereaux. "Tell me what happened. Where are your servants?"

"Today is my assistant's day off, which is why I arranged for our appointment today. I thought he'd be more comfortable with them gone. It was Cook who I sent off to summon the gendarmes." With our appearance he seemed less frantic and more worried. "Anticipating your arrival soon, and not hearing him stir above me— my office is under his bedroom— I made my way up here to remind him of our appointment. I thought him sulking, and I put his delay in coming down to his reluctance in wanting this meeting that I had urged upon him."

"Was the door unlocked? Open or closed? And the curtains?"

"The door was unlocked but closed. When he didn't respond to my knock, I opened it. The curtains were closed, making the room too dark for a proper examination, so I opened them for more light."

"Is the room as you found it otherwise?"

"Yes. Other than the body and drapes, I touched nothing."

"Good."

Charlotte withdrew a pocket handkerchief from her coat's inner pocket, and using it, lifted a drinking glass that was on the washstand. She sniffed it and then brought it to me. Recognizing the smell, we exchanged a knowing look.

I asked, "Was it his habit to take something to go to sleep?"

Dr. Devereaux shrugged. "I hardly know. The man's nightly ritual was his own."

"So you prescribed no sleeping powders for him?"

"No. He never mentioned a need for them to me."

Charlotte said, "Unfortunately, we are very familiar with this scent. For those in a healthy state it puts the user into a cationic state which resembles death. For the dying, it does other things."

We all looked at the figure lying on the bed. He said, "So you think—?"

Charlotte said promptly, "This is only my opinion, but I do not think he is dead. His body smells too sweet. His skin is still elastic. The hands have kept some muscle tension."

Dr. Devereaux shook his head. "Imagine something that would put a man so deeply under that his own body no longer shows the signs of life! No wonder he feared being buried alive."

"I fear he is about to be dead if we do not intervene. As a Ghost Talker, I'm trained to sense the energy of the dead— so conversely, we also sense that of the living. And I tell you that Mysir Boutin is a candle, a flickering candle, that is about to go out. We must act quickly if we wish to save him."

"Can we not induce vomiting? I have an emetic here. Or should we take him to a hospital and pump his stomach?"

I looked at Charlotte for an answer.

"From the state of his bedclothes, I think he took this prior to bed. That would put it what? Five, maybe eight hours ago? From my experience with this concoction it enters the bloodstream relatively quickly. It is difficult, nay almost impossible, to wake someone from it. We will need to wait until its hold on him starts to wane. We could risk injecting a stimulant, but that could also kill him."

I said, "I would like to try something. If his soul is traveling to the Beyond, I could bring him back. That could wake him and be less dangerous." Twyla had done this very thing. Perhaps I could also?

Devereaux simply asked, "What do you need?"

"A stool or chair. Matches. Something that will hold a burning coal." These were all swiftly arranged to my satisfaction, and as he did so, I unpacked my case. I had learned long ago to bring it to all of my appointments, as you never knew what a client would request or what spirits you might find.

To Devereaux, I said, "I have not had time to explain my work to you, but in brief, there are three planes of existence. The earthly where the living resides; the Beyond, where ghosts reside; and the Afterlife. Upon our death, we may go to either the Beyond, where we wait, or to the Afterlife."

A doubt in the back of my mind told me I couldn't achieve this, but I squelched it. I had no time now for what-ifs. A man's life was at stake, so I would try what I could. "I shall go into the Beyond with my mind and see if I can find Mysir Boutin. The goal is to reunite him here with his physical body. Let us hope he has not strayed to the Afterlife, for that is a place I cannot go."

Using the low footstool that Dr. Devereaux supplied, I arranged myself at the side of the bed. Mysir Boutin's hand sported a band of gold that held an onyx stone. The ring was deeply embedded in his finger's flesh and was not something he could have removed easily.

Picking up his cool hand in my warm one, I indicated the ring to Dr. Devereaux. "Does he always wear this?"

"Yes. It was the only piece of jewelry I saw him wear on a regular basis."

Perhaps I could use the connection as Twyla had with me and my father's watch. Hopefully, it would serve as a guide.

The coal burning in the ashtray that Dr. Devereaux had brought me was starting to turn white. I sprinkled some herbs on top and waved the resulting smoke gently into my nostrils.

"Is there anything for us to do?" asked Charlotte.

"Hm. It will appear that I am in a sleep or a deep meditation. Do not disturb it. Even if the gendarmes arrives while I am under, let me finish and come out of my trance naturally. If he fades any more, Charlotte will need to try her method."

Charlotte asked Dr. Devereaux if he had what she needed in his office and he left to quickly return with a few bottles and a hypodermic needle. Setting it aside on the table, she pulled out her pocket watch and took the wrist of our patient. In a moment she met my eyes and shook her head. "Because I'm looking for it. I catch it occasionally, but his pulse is very faint and fluttering. He's under deep. You best work fast if you think there's a chance of bringing him back. Otherwise I'm going to try my method."

Bringing Boutin awake would do no good if he had no soul. It was time to get to work.

Chapter Fourteen

This was the first time I'd returned to the Beyond for months, except for that brief stint during the episode at the Luminary. In a strange way, I found that I had missed the place.

The gray nothingness was perhaps easiest to describe as a heavy fog. But it did not smell of the sea like my home in Alenbonné, or of anything else for that matter. The Beyond was a null place, absent of the textures the earthly plane offered.

Unlike Parnell Lafayette, who had wanted to erect a palace here, I was very careful to keep my mind blank. I did not want to bring anything here that did not belong, nor create a reality like the tiara dragon had done from my memories.

Instead, I focused on the ring and its owner, seeking that bond we create between ourselves and those well-loved, long-owned possessions. I would have liked to credit my ability as a Ghost Talker to why it worked, but I suspect that the three soul-sisters were the reason. In a short time, I was standing outside an office front with the name Roux & Sons written in gold on a green sign-board above the door.

The latch opened easily under my hand and inside I found the man who was Dr. Devereaux's resident patient. Alive, his face took on the vibrancy that the slack one on the bed had not. He had rather a high color in his cheeks, and a pale brow. Upon seeing me he pursed his lips tightly as if he was sucking on a lemon, forming deep brackets on either side of his nose.

"Do I have the pleasure of meeting Mysir Boutin? Or is it Roux?" I asked.

"And who the devil, may I ask, wants to know my business?" the man demanded, rising from behind a desk where he had been looking through ledger books. His accent surprised me. He was from Perino. This was not something the doctor had mentioned, and I had not thought to ask.

"I am Madame Elinor Chalamet, and I hope to be of service to you, Mysir Roux." I used the name on the door, playing a hunch. Often the Beyond revealed a truth that was concealed on the living plane. "I am an associate of Dr. Devereaux. You may recall that we were to have a consultation to discuss your fears about dying."

In animation, Mysir Boutin-Roux had the mien of a man who blustered in order to hide his inadequacies. However, despite the faux outrage he displayed at my appearance, he was nervous. At my words, he licked his lips and cast a glance over his shoulder before replying. "My fears? What would I have to fear?"

Being a Ghost Talker required patience; you couldn't push or rush things. However, we were working against time. The drug could kill him and make his residency here permanent.

"You took a dangerous drug, and it has put you in a state close to death."

His eyes swiveled again, back and forth, as he lied. "I don't know what you are talking about, young lady. Now, if you would be good enough to go." His hand flicked a shooing gesture at me as he took a step back around his desk.

I pressed forward. "The drug you took puts the body into a

sleeping death. If I don't help you back to the earthly plane, you might find that the sleeping part becomes permanent. Do you want to live? If not, I shall indeed go."

Some of my words seemed to finally penetrate his thick head. "Asleep? I can't be! As you see, I'm working."

Indeed, we stood in what looked like an office that you might find down at the docks. There were wood file cabinets, a captain's chair, and a very solid-looking desk. Accounting ledgers were all in a row on the bookshelves. However, I knew these to be nothing but an illusion. Like the conservatory that the dragon had created — or the palace built out of Parnell Lafayette's mind. They weren't real. These images were from Boutin, or Roux's mind, but memories were always flawed.

"Look out the window and tell me what you see. Or better, go out to the street."

He stepped past me and jerked open the door, rattling the bell that hung at the top. Beyond was nothing but the gray mist of the Beyond. The street he probably expected to see did not exist here, for he would have to think it into being and hold that image in his mind constantly.

He spun about, his eyes frightened, as he rushed forward and grabbed my shoulder. "What have you done? Where is the Rue Escoffier? What have you done with it?"

I backhanded his hand off my shoulder and stepped out of his reach. "I have done nothing. You are in a dream state. A land without boundaries. A figment of your mind."

He gave another nervous lick, his stare growing more frantic. I needed to calm him down.

"What is the last thing you remember before coming here?"

"Working, of course! An ordinary day at the office."

I cocked my head. "Truly?"

He paused, visibly struggling to remember. "No. I had— had a bath."

"Where?"

"In my apartment."

"That is where?"

"At Dr. Devereaux's." As the words slipped out, his eyes widened as the words connected him back with his memory.

I nodded in satisfaction. "Now, the stuff you drank before bedtime. Is that something you usually take?"

"It's from my doctor. My medical doctor. Prescribed. I picked up my last dose about a month ago. Before I came to Dr. Devereaux's house."

"Are you ill, mysir? Close to death from sickness?"

"No! No. Why would think that?"

"Because this medicine is used to extend the life of the dying. If well, it puts you into a deep trance akin to death, sending your soul here to the Beyond, the realm we now occupy. A land for ghosts, not the living."

His mouth gaped like a fish before he regained enough of his composure to snap, "I use it to sleep. Nothing more."

"Was this dose from a new or old bottle?"

"A new one. I had some of the old stuff left and used it first before opening the last one I picked up from the chemist."

What a fool! He runs off to Devereaux to hide his whereabouts, but returns to his old chemist! How easy to blame his death on an 'overdose' of a dangerous drug, with no one being the wiser of it being a planned murder.

"Did you find this a stronger dose than usual? Did it smell different? Taste stronger?" The expression on his face told me I was correct. "I believe someone tampered with your medicine. They want you dead, mysir. Do you have any idea who that would be?"

He blustered, his eyes doing their sideways dance. "Kill me? Why? I'm just a merchant! Why would someone want to harm me over a bundle of wool?"

"A very rich merchant, or so I'm told. I wonder how you accumulated those riches?"

His face paled at my words. He would have grabbed me again, but I stepped away, putting the desk between us. I had thwarted an ancient dragon and a serial killer in the Beyond. I wasn't going to be abused by a fat wool merchant here.

"What do you know?"

I didn't know much, but I was beginning to suspect a lot. The drug was being used by the mastermind to put people under his control. Or to remove enemies.

"You angered the wrong person, mysir. He will hunt you down and dispose of you like a housekeeper does a mouse unless you make a friend of the cat. I am that cat. Be truthful with me and I will save you."

He had to trust me if he wanted out of here.

"Yes, you are right. My real name is Roux. I am also a wool merchant. Exporter actually. I buy the wool clips and then ship it to Perino. I have family contacts there."

"Go on. There's more to this story than sheep."

"Well. Import taxes in Sarnesse are pretty high! Merchants are being robbed! So I'd smuggle a few things into Alenbonné from Perino, where I have family. Personal things. Nothing that the king or his tax collectors should care about."

"Like what?" I pressed.

"Oh, just a few luxury goods. Coffee, chocolate, silks. Small things."

"But small things became big things, did they not?"

His face sagged, collapsing like a straw man losing his stuffing. "Someone noticed what I was doing. I think it was one of my dock hands. A stranger approached me, and he promised to reward me if I just looked the other way. There was no chance of saying no, you understand. Every time I did what he wanted, a bag of coins appeared in my desk drawer on a regular schedule."

"What was it they wanted you to move? Was it in or out?"

"Small things went out. Jewels and gold bars. I wasn't

supposed to look, you understand, but a bag broke and it spilled out."

Oh, I bet it did! Spilled right into his hands and bank account!

"It was what they were bringing in that made me nervous." He wrung his hands like a nervous woman, his eyes widening to show more white. "I thought a peek wouldn't matter. I wasn't going to tell anyone. Who would I tell?"

"And what did you see?"

"Guns. Lots of guns."

That surprised me. "Why smuggle those? They aren't illegal in Sarnesse."

"Arms are to be licensed, and there is a limit on what can be brought in. There were a lot, and they had a strange design, like nothing I had seen before." He swallowed hard. "About a month after I noticed the guns, they stopped asking me, so I thought they were done."

A smuggling operation shutting down because they were done? They were done with something— with him!

"But that wasn't true, was it?"

"No. The gendarmes found my warehouse manager dead in a canal. The story was that he had taken too much drink and probably fallen in. I knew that wasn't true, for the man hated the smell of liquor. A teetotaler. Next, one of my accountants, who helped me with the books, didn't come in. When I sent someone around to her lodging, they found her swinging from a beam. I knew I was next. They were sweeping away anyone who knew about them."

"And so you ran? With their money?"

For a moment he looked affronted. "Do you think that wasn't my money with the risks I took? Two of my employees dead, my business to be abandoned? They owed me!"

I highly doubted that the thieves saw it that way.

"I think you've been involved in a very complex criminal scheme, Mysir Roux. If you were to provide a friend of mine with information about these people, I think he can safeguard you."

"If I am here in this strange place, then they have found me. Tried to kill me with my medicine. There is no hope for me. I'm a dead man walking."

The bell on the door rang, and we both turned to see Sergeant Quincy Dupont enter.

CHAPTER FIFTEEN

The shock of seeing him made me as dumb as a lamppost. He was wearing his guardia uniform, with braid and badges. Clean-shaven, eyes alert, his hat cocked sideways. He looked brighter than I had ever seen him.

Dupont addressed a question to Roux. "I have been checking my notes and I have one more question for you, mysir. When did you last see my sister?"

The shock of seeing the sergeant in a place I least expected him stunned me.

In an angry voice, Roux snapped, "As I've told you many times, I know nothing about her!"

"I know she was working for you," Dupont insisted.

"As many other girls do in the warehouse. That doesn't mean I know them. Talk to my manager if you need information."

The sergeant moved his bulk closer to Roux, looking him scornfully up and down. "I have. He told me that Meike was often called to your private office. Why did you single her out?"

At the utterance of this name, one of my soul ladies stirred. I had a horrible sinking feeling about the fate of Sergeant Dupont's sister.

"Who is your superior officer? I wish to lodge a complaint," stuttered Roux, flustered. But he was no match for Dupont, who, for the first time in my acquaintance with him, was acting like a man instead of a sack.

From a lifeless, rather dull character, his face was now flushed with anger, eyes alive with intelligence. The animation gave a completely different cast to his face. Before it had looked like unrisen dough, and now it looked like a man spoiling for a fight. If someone had asked me to explain what I was seeing, I would have insisted that he must have a twin.

"Have you harmed her?" growled the sergeant. He was so close that his face was only inches away from the merchant's nose.

And even more puzzling, he had never expressed an interest in the Spirit realm. How had he traveled here?

"Sergeant Dupont!" I cried, but had to repeat myself several times before he turned his attention to me. "Perhaps I can help get you the answer, if you answer some questions of my own."

"You? Who are you? His woman?"

I ignored the insult. "Don't you recognize me? I'm Madame Chalamet? Elinor Chalamet. I work with your superior, Inspector Barbier."

He shook his head vehemently. "You are mistaken, madame. I don't know him. My commanding officer is Lapointe. That is who I answer to."

I frowned. It was not uncommon for the dead, for ghosts and souls, to forget facts. The Beyond clouds the mind; even Roux had not remembered, until prompted, where he had been last. Dupont was alive as far as I knew. Perhaps even working with a Ghastly to cause trouble.

But was he instead somehow dead? It would explain his presence here. I asked, "Does Lapointe know you are here?"

He physically drew back from both of us, his spine stiffening. "Lapointe would agree I should investigate this matter of my missing sister."

"But you have not consulted him? You are here on your own? To find out more about Meike?"

He gave a curt nod to each of my points, then pointed a beefy finger at Roux. "Are you acquainted with this man?"

"Not really. I was to be introduced, but that did not happen. I was told his name was Mysir Boutin."

Sergeant Dupont said abruptly, "His real name is Roux. My half-sister worked for him, washing and carding his wool to prepare it for the market. That is until she didn't come home. She was barely eighteen! It would be best if you do not involve yourself with this man. He is a scoundrel."

"I tell you I know nothing about what happened to the girl!" interjected Roux.

I was on Dupont's side. Roux was not to be trusted. "Start being honest!" I snapped. "Or I won't help you return to your body."

"Body?" repeated Dupont. This made me think that like Roux, he really didn't know where he was.

"We are in the Beyond," I explained to him. "The realm of ghosts. I am Madame Elinor Chalamet, a Ghost Talker. Whether you remember me, I know you in the real world of flesh and blood. I've worked on several murder cases with you and your superior, Inspector Barbier, so why you don't remember that, and how you got here, is a puzzle. To untangle this, I must ask you some questions. Did your sister ever mention a man, Parnell Lafayette, to you? Or express any interest in the Morpheus Society? Or in the spiritual realm of ghosts?"

Perhaps because I expressed an interest in his sister and might provide answers, Dupont answered my questions eagerly. "She was curious about spirits and such. Always loved scary stories and wanted to meet a ghost."

"What do you know of Parnell Lafayette, Mysir Roux?" I demanded. "For he developed that 'medicine' you took. He used it to put a person into a trance state so they could travel the ghostly Beyond as they hovered between life and death."

His short-fingered hands clasped each other as if they wanted to hold on to something for reassurance. Between me and Dupont, he stood no chance, and he knew it, so he started giving a rushed confession. "The name is familiar. Yes. Yes. I met him at some parties. He told me he had something that would calm me down, help me to not be so nervous and anxious. But it wouldn't be addictive, like zhimo."

Those damn parties again!

"At these parties, did young girls go into a sleeping state? Did ghosts appear as if they were real?"

"You've been?" Before I could explain that I only knew of them third-hand, he continued. "I don't care for ghosts or the dead. Nothing like that. But the people I told you about earlier, my business acquaintances, they invited me. It was interesting, so I kept going."

Drugs and young girls for the taking? I'm sure he did find it delightful!

"Did you take Mys Meike Roord to one of these parties?"

Before he could speak, his face revealed the truth, and Dupont pounced. The Dupont I knew had been near a vegetable, dull, non-questioning, compliant. In fact, not a man of action, but one that was directed. But here he was no dummy. No placid cow, but a fiery bull. In a flash, he lunged and had Roux on his tiptoes. The man's body arced in pain as the sergeant twisted his arm behind his back.

"Where is my sister?" Dupont growled. "Did you take her to these debaucheries? Sell her?"

Roux whined in a high, breathless voice, "Yes, I admit it. She wanted to go to talk with the ghosts. The last time I saw her was there. But I don't know where she is now and had nothing to do with whatever happened to her. I swear!"

If Dupont broke Roux's arm in the Beyond, would Roux's

living body also have a broken arm? An interesting experiment, but we had better things to concentrate on now.

"If you will release him, sergeant, I think I can tell you the fate of your sister."

Dupont relaxed his hold a little on Roux, but did not let him go completely. Would any brother? "Go on."

"I'm afraid it is not good news. A man called Parnell Lafayette of the Morpheus Society developed an elixir— a mix of narcotics — and gave it to young girls to put them in a state between life and death. He used them like mules to carry him into the Beyond. The place we are now, where ghosts reside, between the earthly plane and the Afterlife."

"Tell me where this Lafayette is," Dupont said. He jerked upward on Roux's arm, causing the wool merchant to give a breathless scream of pain.

"He is dead." I really hoped Parnell did not wander into the shop as a ghost; none of us needed that complication. I added slowly, "As, I fear, your sister is."

His arms fell away from Roux, who stumbled against his desk, trying to regain his balance. Dupont seemed shocked, disbelieving, like most are after receiving such devastating news. Hope is always the last to die.

"She can't be. I'd have seen her at the morgue. Or heard about it. I would know being a guardia."

He was deluding himself. Alenbonné was big enough and in places, dark enough, that bodies could vanish, never to be seen again.

"I don't know where her physical body is but her spirit, her soul, I found in the Beyond when Parnell brought me to his place here. She helped me stop him. She is here now. Would you like to see her?"

He nodded, numb and confused.

I could restrain her no longer, my soul-sister with the deep music of a cello. She surfaced as a gold column, illuminating the dingy offices with a blazing glow. As her body formed from the sparkles, the men gazed upon her in wonder, for she was uncanny and beautiful.

Perhaps it was the time we had spent together, or the strength of her spirit. Or perhaps it was seeing her brother again that gave her the power to control my mouth. She made me say, in a tone quite unlike my own, "Quincy."

"Meike?"

"It is time you knew the truth, my dear brother. Mysir Roux did take me to the party, but I begged to go. It was there that I met Lafayette Parnell. He knew some of what I wanted to learn. He took me on as an apprentice."

"Meike!" he cried out, this time in admonition.

"I know. I know, brother! So foolish. But I am headstrong, and he promised me. Promised me!" My voice vibrated with passion and anger.

"How came you to be here? With this woman? Who is she?"

"After he murdered me, Lafayette held my soul in the Beyond to provide the energy he needed for his sick fantasy. Elinor helped me. Us. But enough of my story. You are the one that is in danger, my dear one. Listen, my brother, while I can still use her to speak with you. You are sundered. Your soul's lifeline to your body is no more. There is no going back. No hope of returning to life."

"I don't know what you mean," he said in surprise, blinking rapidly. "Of course I'm alive! I'm talking to you right now."

"Observe." She waved her golden arm towards Roux and suddenly a twisted silver rope became visible. One end entered the space in his chest right above his heart and the other end snaked away, sliding out the door, into the void. "Mysir Roux still has an anchor to his body. He can return. As Elinor can."

From the corner of my eye I saw another silver rope from my chest, right where the watch had marked me, spin out, going through the office door. Into the grayness, back to my physical body.

Dupont had no similar thread.

"You are nothing but soul," Meike said. "Another possesses your flesh and you cannot return to it."

"Meike," he said for the third time. "I don't understand. I can't be dead."

"Your body is not dead, but you cannot go back to a house that is occupied," she explained to him patiently.

Dupont possessed? Had that happened by accident or by design? If planned, why? Considering Dupont's lack of knowledge about me and Barbier, it seemed that whatever had caused his soul to separate had happened some time ago.

Thinking of my interactions with him, I shivered. What had been looking out of his eyes?

"Brother. Do you trust me? Give me your hands." He nodded dumbly and held out his strong, square hands, putting them into her golden ones. "Let us go home. Together."

No! I tried protesting. Surely there was some way I could help Dupont regain his body. But even as that thought crossed my mind, I knew that with the strand of life broken, there was no repairing it. I could feel Meike pushing my soul aside as her connection pulled away from me. My two remaining soul-sisters released her easily enough, but for me it was as if we were glued sheets of paper. As she left, it tore me. Part of me gone with her, part of her remaining.

She broke free. Without her, I collapsed to my knees, trying to catch my breath. My chest felt tight. The floor beneath me floated and started to spin.

As she joined her soul with that of her brother, his mouth opened in astonishment, his eyes seeing wonder. Dupont's body sparkled with gold twinkling light as they merged into one and then became two lights. One gold, one silver, both shooting off rainbow prisms as they twirled together.

It was beautiful and terrifying at the same time.

The deep cello that was Meike Roord's soul song changed,

becoming a duet with her brother's drum. The sound pulsated around us, growing louder, making a heartbeat. In a flash, they became an exploding rainbow before their lights vanished.

Tears trailing down my face, I told Roux, "It is time we go home. There is nothing here for us now."

CHAPTER SIXTEEN

Returning to the earthly plane was a shock. Not only had I lost another soul sister and was feeling the heartache of it, but I awoke from my trance to a room filled with gendarmes.

"Give her some room, boys. She doesn't need you all breathing down her neck," said Inspector Barbier.

Dr. Devereaux pressed a glass into my hand, bringing it to my lips, I found it to be sherry. In a quiet voice, he asked me, "Are you all right?"

I nodded and cleared my throat to greet Barbier. "Hello, inspector, when did you get here?"

"I was told to hurry over here, as there was a dead body."

Charlotte was still holding the merchant's wrist, and now she placed it back on the bed. "Sorry to disappoint you, but I think he's coming around now."

True to her word, Roux groaned and, opening his eyes, struggled to sit up in bed. The three gendarmes crowding around his bed to see the body might have been why he gave a stifled scream. He pulled the covers up over his head and from under them exclaimed in a muffled voice, "Why are all these people in my room?! Get them out!"

I took another drink, slowly feeling some life return. Still, my head seemed disconnected from my body and watched the proceedings with a remote clinical interest.

"Thank you for coming so promptly, but it looks like we won't need you after all," said Dr. Devereaux dryly.

Barbier shrugged his narrow shoulders. "Makes a pleasant break for us. We were in the neighborhood having a discussion with some citizens who thought throwing bricks through rich toff's windows was a fun game. Now I can haul them down to the station instead of wasting time with sick people."

Charlotte had come over to stand by me. Bending down, she asked quietly, "You are all right, aren't you?"

"Yes, I'm fine. Just a little light-headed."

Barbier snapped his fingers and pointed to the door, causing his three men to fall into a formation. I heard their boots clattering down the stairs. When Barbier made a move to follow, I cried, "Wait. If you have a moment, may I speak with you?"

Casting a glance between Dr. Devereaux and Charlotte, he returned his gaze to me and nodded.

"I'll be back in a moment," I assured Charlotte, and went to the landing outside Roux's room. "I know you are busy with what is happening in the city, but I was wondering if you had any time free? Could I come by the station for a visit?"

He rubbed his chin. "Certainly. But why the mystery? Is there something you want? Just ask."

I did not want to discuss what I had found out about Dupont in this haphazard way. That would need time for a proper investigation into how Dupont's soul lost track of his body. However, there was something else I wanted to know right now.

"Why did you take me to Madame Granger after my father's death?"

He showed surprise. "That? That was long ago."

"Yes. But I was just wondering if you knew her personally? What the connection was? Why you thought of her in particular?"

He pulled on his earlobe, thinking. "I'd heard of her. Someone said she worked with those who were grieving. I can't remember if it was someone at the station or in the neighborhood. It was too long ago. Of course, I didn't believe all that ghost talking stuff back then, but in the end you convinced me." He gave me a wry smile.

"Did you know she needed an apprentice? That she would take me on?"

"Never. I just thought she'd give you some advice and let you talk about your dad. You could have knocked me over with a feather when she said to bring your things to her house, and that she wanted to look after you."

His hand slid down on the banister rail as if he was ready to leave.

"Thank you. I was pretty lost in my grief. I'm not sure what I would have done except for you and Leona."

He gave me an awkward pat on my shoulder. "Now, look, don't get maudlin on me. You were such a small lost thing; what could I do? What you need right now is a good murder. It would cheer you right up."

"Well, next time you get one, let me know and I'll come Ghost Talk it."

He grinned. "That's the spirit! Now, I must get those boys down to the station with their catch or they'll wander off looking for lunch at a diner or a food cart."

I bade him goodbye and returned to the room. Charlotte and Dr. Devereaux were arguing with Roux. It seemed the merchant wanted to leave. "You told me my apartments would be private!"

Dr. Devereaux was far more patient than I would have been in the situation. "That was before I found you looking dead. Surely you understand why I had to make a call for help?"

Moving over to the window, I looked down and saw Barbier exit the house. Outside was a guardia custody wagon. From his gestures, he was ordering his men to climb aboard so they could leave. They did not seem very quick to obey, and Barbier used his hat to knock one of them upside the head to get him to move faster.

He probably wished he had Dupont at hand to help. But he never would again. This thought made me sad, and I turned away.

Roux was tucking his nightshirt into the top of his trousers. "I will leave immediately, doctor. You have not provided the security that you told me you would."

"I'm sorry, Mysir Boutin, but you must understand why."

"It's actually Mysir Roux," I interjected, causing the merchant to exclaim his outrage. "How could you! That was told in confidence." He came over to me and shook his finger in my face.

"You can hardly expect me to keep quiet about you smuggling guns."

At that moment, there was a tinkling of glass and we both swiveled our necks to see that the windowpane had cracked. Across the street there was a reflection like that of a mirror aimed at the sun's rays.

"What?!" exclaimed Dr. Devereaux.

Charlotte shouted, "Get down, Elinor!"

I stared uncomprehendingly while a second glass broke and blood bloomed on the chest of the white shirt of Mysir Roux.

He fell like one pole-axed to the ground. Charlotte grabbed my wrist and swung me away from the window to the wall. She held me in a vise-like clasp. "The curtains, Armand! Close those damn curtains!"

On his hands and knees, Devereaux scurried to the window, pulling the drapes together and shielding the room from an outside view. The broken glass on the carpet sliced his hands, so they were bleeding as he went to the second window facing the street and closed them as well.

Only then did Charlotte let me go so we could check on Roux.

It didn't take a moment to examine him and know that he was truly gone. Charlotte gave the pronouncement.

"The man's dead. Shot through the heart and lung."

I ran to the bed and started hastily packing my things into my bag. Removing my man-stopper from an interior pocket, I loaded it. "Dr. Devereaux, is there a way to get out of your house without being seen?"

"Do you think whoever did this is coming here?!" he cried out, alarmed.

"No. I think they got what they wanted. But I need to get out of here immediately. I have important information I need to share with the duke de Archambeau."

"What information? Who?" Dr. Devereaux sounded bewildered.

"Just answer her," Charlotte said sharply.

Looking at her and then back at me, he told me, "There's a way out through the kitchen. We have a small yard and a coal shed that opens to a back alley."

Holding the gun in one hand and my bag in the other, I asked, "Which way should I go to catch a cab?"

"Go right. It will eventually dead-end into the Rue Principale. Take a left. There is a train station a few blocks down and the cabs are often there looking for passengers."

"Thank you." At the door, I told Charlotte, "Search the room. Especially look for any journals or letters. Tristan will want them."

Charlotte nodded. Before I could step out of the room, she was already stripping Roux's bed, looking for evidence.

Down stairs, in the foyer, I took a moment to lock the front door. From there I went down a narrow hall and found a door at the back, which led into the kitchen.

Devereaux's cook, who was peeling potatoes, said sharply, "Now here! Who you be?"

"Sorry, madame. I am a guest of your master. I'm leaving out the back with his permission." My hand was already on the handle of the door that led to the yard, but I paused. "Do you have an umbrella anywhere close, by chance?"

Obviously puzzled by my request since it was a clear day, she pointed to a corner of the room. Grabbing the one propped against the wall, I popped it open, and placing it over my head, exited to the yard.

I kept the umbrella up, using it to shield me from anyone looking for a target from above. It was merely a precaution, as the shooter must have been located across the street to have shot through Roux's window. They were probably still there, ready to cause more trouble, or in the process of leaving. I hoped that the direction of their exit would not be the same as mine.

A woman in skirts cannot move quickly enough when she fears being shot at. Picking them up, I did as best as I could while juggling the case, umbrella, and gun.

Where the alley ended was the Rue Principale. There were a few people about, so I dropped my skirt as to not draw attention, but kept my pace as quick as I feasibly could without appearing to be a thief or a maniac.

"You!" I shouted at a quick-cab driver who was just mounting back up to his seat. "Are you available?"

"Yes, madame."

Before he could step down and help me, I hopped in, slamming the flap over my legs. I gave him the address for Hartwood House and settled the umbrella in front of me, making it screen me from those in the street.

From above the driver told me, "Might be hard to get over that way, madame."

"Triple the fee, if you can get me at least close enough to walk."

"For that, I'll get you to the door."

CHAPTER SEVENTEEN

Tristan's footman, Ruben, escorted me without a word to the drawing room where Valentina was working on a watercolor of a fruit bowl. Seeing me, she stood up, brush in hand, her hands stained with color.

"Ruben, would you find my tea? It's overdue. See if my brother has finished his meeting and if so, ask him to come here."

Ruben bowed out and closed the door. Valentina set down her brush, and coming to me, took the umbrella from my hand. Closing it, she set it aside. Next, she put my case on a table before leading me to a sofa.

"Is the blood yours, Elinor?"

"Blood?"

She pointed, and I looked down. My jacket, gaping open, showed the front of my blouse splattered with red drying to brown.

"I think that was from Mysir Roux. When they shot him."

"I see."

A servant rolled a tea trolley into the room. The servant gave me an intense stare before lowering her eyes. Valentina shooed her away. "A couple of hot water bottles and a warm wet cloth. Quickly."

The girl left and Valentina finished bringing the cart to where I was trying not to smear blood on her cushions. She poured me a cup of tea but when she started to put honey into it, causing me to protest, "Just lemon."

"I think you need the honey for now." She handed me the cup, then pulled a throw off the back of a chair and settled it over my lap and chest.

"The blood!" I warned her. "Don't get it stained. It's so pretty."

"Don't worry about that."

She was wearing a plain dress covered with a light blue apron that was daubed with paint stains. This was the most approachable I had ever seen her look. I liked this Valentina much better than the cold socialite.

"Aren't you going to ask what happened? Why I am here?"

"We can talk about that when you are ready."

It was a different servant who returned. Valentina took the hot water bottles from her and, one by one, slipped them under my blanket. My stiff hands crept over them, seeking warmth. The girl handed Valentina a wet cloth, and she used it to pat my aching face. When she laid it back down, it was pink.

"Is Tristan here? It's terribly important that I see him as soon as possible."

"He's here, but he's in a meeting with Mysir de Windt and Lady Talleyrand. I will make sure he sees you as soon as he is free." She poured me a second cup of tea and put in more honey. "Now, finish this one too, and then have one of these egg salad bread fingers."

I took one, nibbling the end. "I really need to see Tristan."

"I know dear. You will, I promise."

"It's terribly important," I said around the food.

"I'm sure it is," she said soothingly.

"Why doesn't he come? He's never where I need him!" I cried, my voice becoming a little hysterical to my ears. As if my words had rubbed a magic lamp, Tristan entered the room.

Valentina stood up to greet him. "There you are. Elinor has had a shock, Tristan, so do treat her kindly and be circumspect with using your usual sarcastic wit." With that, she left us alone.

By this time he had come around the sofa and seen my face. I wasn't sure what was wrong with it, but he went pale and immediately sat down beside me. "What happened, Elinor? Are you all right?"

"I'm all right, but why didn't you come? I sent you a note. You should have come."

"You're right, I should have," he said gently. "But you see, I didn't know it was an emergency. Where is Farrow?"

"I don't know. Probably back at Dr. Devereaux's residence. If you had been with me, none of this would have happened. You would have been smart enough to close the drapes. Were you sulking because I said no to your proposal?"

"I was busy trying to save Sarnesse, but perhaps there was a bit of sulking, too. Now tell me what happened."

Where to start?

"Twyla came home. She visited me with Leona and Leona said I should retire. That I hadn't any talent and should get married. Do you think that? Is that why you proposed to me? Because I'm not talented enough to look after myself?"

"Not at all. Is Twyla hurt? Where is she?"

"She wasn't with me today," I said impatiently. Wasn't he following? "She left a note with Anne-Marie and it said she knew something about my father, but when I tried to see her, she wasn't available. I think Leona is keeping her from me. Or is she keeping Twyla for herself? She says there have been complaints about me. Unofficial complaints that could cause me to be expelled from the Morpheus Society."

Tristan's eyes were very serious. "Where is she? Should I get her?"

"She's at Leona's house, but no, don't do that. I'm not sure what is going on yet, but I've set Marcus to finding out. If Twyla really wanted out of there, she would have said that."

"So you didn't come here about Twyla?"

"I didn't. But it's all part of this strange week when you didn't reply to my note and ignored me to sulk. Like what happened yesterday, when I had to run away from the gendarmes with Theodoor Vischeer."

"Vischeer? The naturalist?"

"Yes. He took me to a diner with horrible food. If that is what the workers have to eat during the day, no wonder they are striking and want better money. It was greasy and unpleasant. He told me that his friend was a member of the Brotherhood. They are going to do something— blow things up or shoot people— not me, just people in government like you. I wasn't sure exactly as he was vague, but it didn't seem to be good for anyone and he wants you to stop it."

"I thought Vischeer was part of the Brotherhood," said Tristan, meditatively. By this time his hand had come under the throw and was covering mine. It was much nicer than a hot water bottle.

"Yes, although he said it more like he knew of them, though I think he is a card-carrying member, if they had cards."

"Elinor, what did Vischeer want me to do?"

"He wants a meeting, or his group does, with some official. He said the king, but he can't be serious. His Majesty is too busy stuffing himself with cake and wine to do anything as serious as that! So I imagine you'll have to find someone to talk to him. He wants to expand the number in the House of Commons to appease the Brotherhood so they don't overthrow the government."

"Was it Vischeer who hurt you?" His fingers came up but did not touch my cheek.

"No. That was someone else with a gun. It's probably one of those special guns that Roux said he smuggled in from Perino. He said they were unusual and don't you think it would take a special gun to shoot across a street from one building to another? That's not an ordinary rifle. He had to shoot twice, and have it go through a windowpane, so I think that is pretty good, considering."

"Who is Roux?" asked Tristan, pronouncing each word very carefully.

"Haven't you been listening? Tristan, please don't make me revise my opinion of your intelligence. I simply can't be in a relationship with a man who lacks wits. Not only would it harm my reputation, but I would find it deadly dull."

Looking chastised, he told me, "I promise I will try to do better. Now, who is Roux? You have not mentioned him before."

"He's Dr. Devereaux's patient."

"Who is Dr. Devereaux?"

"A friend of Charlotte's. Not exactly a friend, but work colleagues. They belong to the same club and he told her about a patient who feared being buried alive. Charlotte recommended that he consult with me because she thought I could reassure him. Devereaux is a mind doctor, an alienist."

"Ah."

"Yes, that explains everything, doesn't it? I was to meet him today, but when I got to Devereaux's house, Roux was dead."

"He was shot?"

"How am I going to tell you this story if you keep interrupting me with your silly questions? No. He was only a little dead, for he had taken Parnell's drug, which we really should give a name to. I went into the Beyond to bring him back to his body, and that's when he told me about the gun smuggling. Or was that after Sergeant Dupont showed up? I think that was before?"

Things were very hard to explain when you needed to keep all the details straight.

"Sergeant Dupont was in the Beyond?"

"That's what I asked myself! How did he get there? It's because of his dead sister, Meike Roord. One of the four souls that Parnell used for his sick fantasy of living in the Beyond as a method to extend his life without taking the drug himself. She's not inside me anymore because she took her brother's soul to the Afterlife."

"So Sergeant Dupont is dead? When did this happen?"

I shook my head. "No! No! He's not dead! His body is still here, walking around. The connection between his soul and body was severed and now something else is using his body. And I thought the Ghastlys were bad enough!"

"Ghastlys?"

"That's what Charlotte calls these people."

Tristan leaned sideways onto the couch in a half-collapse. "I think I'm catching up. Twyla is being held under house arrest by Madame Granger. Mysir Vischeer wants to stop the Brotherhood from doing something they can't take back. Dupont's body is walking about somewhere, while his soul took off to the Afterlife with his sister. How does Mysir Roux fit into all of this?"

"He helped the master criminal run guns from Perino into Alenbonné. He tried to keep some gems and gold, but they found out. They killed his manager and his accountant, so he ran away to Devereaux for safety. But he stupidly went to pick up drugs from someone who knew him. I think that's how they traced him to Devereaux's house. They shot him through the window and he bled all over me before he died. Really died. Dead-dead. Then I came here to tell you all about it."

Tristan looked over my head. "Did you two hear all of that?"

"Yes," said de Windt while another softer, female voice replied, "How fascinating."

Part of me wanted to get angry that others had heard what I thought was a private conversation, but I was exhausted. "Good, because I certainly do not want to be repeating myself!"

Lady Talleyrand came and sat in the chair opposite me. She

was wearing a pea green dress with a very simple cut that showed how expensive it was. In her ears were emeralds, but her neck only held a gold chain with an oval locket. Her hair was not all white, as I had previously thought from seeing her in the theater; it was the palest blond that is often so light that it appears so.

She had a well-bred face with several hallmark features which identified her as closely connected to King Guénard's family line. The small ears that lay tight against the head; the nose with that dimpled depression at the end; and her eyes, while not the same color as the king's, did have the same protuberant roundness.

However, she had something Guénard did not— empathy— and this softened her appearance. Her face held a sympathetic kindness to it.

"What a tale of courage and perseverance. By the way, I do not think they have introduced us. I am Lady Maryegold Talleyrand."

"Elinor Chalamet. I am a Ghost Talker."

Her warm smile cast quite the spell; it was no wonder she held a reputation for an ability to calm the most troubled water. To Tristan, who sat next to me, she said, "This Theodoor Vischeer. You know of him? Is he a reliable sort of man? Trustworthy?"

Instead of Tristan, de Windt answered, "We had him down as one of the Brotherhood. Someone near the top of their hierarchy, your ladyship."

"But is he trustworthy?"

Tristan gave his thoughts. "I do not know the man personally, but from the little we have gathered about him, he is intelligent. Whether that is of the cunning variety, I do not know. It is always best to believe the worst and be surprised by the best."

"He *is* sincere," I interjected, since Vischeer was not here to speak for himself.

"Let me discuss this with Guénard and see if he is amenable to such a plan. Perhaps ten more seats would not be amiss and appease them. It would still be well below the number the House of Lords has, enabling them to keep their power."

De Windt protested, appalled, "Your ladyship! Are you seriously considering negotiating with these scum?"

"To bring peace back to Alenbonné, I would carry on a conversation with a diseased rat, if that is what it takes." She said this so pleasantly that it made you wish you could be the rat.

Tristan was thinking about something else. "What concerns me more, de Windt, are these guns. Where are they now? If a meeting with the Brotherhood on neutral ground will cool their tempers until we can find them, that's all for the good. I back Lady Talleyrand's plan for a parley."

"Thank you," she said graciously. "Now, I must leave and prepare for my dinner party. We shall discuss this more fully after I meet with His Majesty." As she stood up, so did Tristan and both men gave her a bow. "De Windt shall escort me back to my residence to insure my safety. And you, my dear boy, shall provide a place for Madame Chalamet to rest and get that wound looked after."

She presented her arm to de Windt, who, being the toady he was, gladly took it with a reverence you would give a queen.

CHAPTER EIGHTEEN

That night, I talked with Twyla in my dreams.

In my mind, we were in my drawing room at the Crown. But, of course, we weren't. Not really.

"Oh madame! I have so much to tell you! Of course, dreams are only one step away from the Beyond, so I thought I might find you here without any snoopers."

We were seated on my sofa, facing each other. "What is going on, Twyla? I stopped by the house twice and they made excuses as to why I could not see you."

She made an exasperated snort. "It's so ridiculous! They are keeping me close because some of the Morpheus members want to steal me away for their own purposes. Use me! Like I would ever let them do that. Madame Granger fears they will kidnap me." She rolled her eyes. "No one can keep me. That's ridiculous!"

"But why couldn't we meet? I would never harm you," I protested.

She clasped my hands tightly and, with our faces close together, said in a hurried rush, "Madame is upset with you. I don't know the whole, but the elders of the Morpheus Society want you out. They've been at her night and day, going on and on about how you have dangerous ideas that could destroy the Society."

Perturbed, I asked, "What ideas?"

"It's all due to Parnell and what happened to him. Several high ups were funding his immortality research, and they feel cheated they did not get the formula. They blame you."

Could this be the girl's overactive imagination? "How do you know this?"

Twyla gave a cluck with her tongue. "By eavesdropping, of course! You didn't think I was going to sit in my room, darning stockings and reading improving literature all day, did you?"

I smiled at that image. "Now that you mention it, that does seem unlikely."

"She fears that if I'm seen as your associate, your reputation will smear mine, so she is keeping us apart. But I think I can drag my reputation in the dirt without any help from you."

Laying a hand on top of the ones in her lap, I patted it in thanks. "Perhaps she is wise in this until we can get things sorted out. Still, remember, if you ever need help, put a handkerchief in the window during the day or a candle at night. Marcus is watching Madame Granger's house and he will know the signal. Once you give us the word, we will storm the house and rescue you!"

Twyla's eyes sparkled with a mischievous gleam. "We? Would that include His Grace? I wouldn't mind seeing him punch Mysir Durant, Madame's man, in the nose. I loved seeing him thrash Parnell."

"I doubt we could stop him from helping. Now quickly, before I wake up and our connection becomes lost. What did you mean by your original note? About my father?"

"He's become a guardian."

This unexpected response made me burst into laughter. It was evidently not what the girl had anticipated, and I could see that my response had irked her. Guardians had long been a myth among the spiritual community; a belief that our loved ones who had traveled all the way to the Afterlife, never to be reached again, could somehow return to guide and protect us. Yes, ghosts in the Beyond can be reached, but those in the Afterlife? No. That was a plane with no communication. I had never seen evidence of anything like that existing in all of my work with spirits.

"Guardians aren't real, Twyla. They are a wish fulfillment by people who want to believe their loved ones are somehow looking after them, warning them, guiding them through life. But we know that once a soul goes to the Afterlife, it is only a one-way trip. There is no coming back."

She said stubbornly, "How can you believe in ghosts but not guardians?"

"I can talk to ghosts, see them, summon them. Guardians? Spirits from the Afterlife that return to the earthly plane? No. All we have are folk tales and incidents that we cannot verify. If a pregnant lady says, 'My mother sent me a dream that I would have a girl,' and then she has a daughter, how is that verification? It is probably hindsight, looking back, filling in the blanks for a narrative that they wish to be true."

Twyla crossed her arms, defensive. "Well, whether you believe me or not, when I was in the Beyond, I had a feeling of a special presence. Not a ghost. And it always happened whenever I thought of you."

Being practical, I tried to give her an explanation she would accept. "Perhaps it was simply a curious ghost? I've communicated with many."

"At first, I thought that as well. But the more I explored it, and tried to get it to speak to me, the more it faded away. It didn't feel like a ghost. It was different, alien, not like a person at all. More like a vibration."

"So why do you think it was my father?" I asked skeptically.

"I wish I had more time to explain this." From her pocket she pulled out a small black notebook. It was the one Inspector

Barbier had gifted her during the Parnell investigation. "I've written more about it in here for you. I'm sure he's crossed back from the Afterlife as a guardian to help you."

"Thank you for the kind thought, my dear, but I think it is unlikely."

There was a knocking in the background of our shared dream. Someone was at the door. A woman's voice, Leona's, was intruding. "Why have you put the chair under the door? What are you doing in there? Let me come in, girl!"

"I must go." She pressed the notepad into my hand. "Read it. I know I'm right. You'll see."

In a blink she was gone, and I too awoke in a strange bed. Oh, now I remembered, I was at Hartwood. My face aching, I struggled to sit up and compose my thoughts. Last night Tristan had sent a note to Anne-Marie and Charlotte letting them know I was there.

Tristan had insisted on carrying me upstairs to a guest room. Using a hand mirror, he'd shown me the gash on my cheek. A traveling bullet had made a path across the skin. After he cleaned the wound, he had applied a sticking plaster. All of this he had done in silence.

After a hot bath, I'd crawled into bed to sleep like the dead.

Last night I had paid little attention to the room, but now I took time to admire it. It wasn't the one that I had had the last time I was here. No, this one had sapphire-blue wallpaper with a wood trim in cream. It must have been a ladies' chamber, for there was a dainty desk for writing letters and a dressing table with a gold-framed wall mirror. There was an enormous wardrobe against one wall and a set of chairs in a baby blue damask.

As I started to get up, I glanced at the table near my bed. Next to my father's watch was a black narrow notebook. Twyla's book.

I slumped back down on the mattress, shocked. I knew the girl could transport herself into the Beyond, but not that she could take objects with her. Transport things to a new location on the earthly plane? She really did have unusual talents. I would have to ask her how that one worked.

Stuffing a pillow behind me, I settled in and reviewed the pages of notes and sketches. Her thoughts on the people she had met made me smile, and I even laughed out loud at her comments about Tristan. Yes, he indeed could be very arrogant!

Before I could get to reading about her visits to the Beyond, there was a tap on the door.

"Come in."

Only after it opened did I realize it was a connecting door between my room and what must have been Tristan's from the masculine decor I glimpsed behind him. He was carrying a breakfast tray.

"This is exceptional room service," I commented. "I'll have to recommend this hotel to all my friends."

"Please don't. I enjoy it being very private and selective."

At his entrance I had pulled the covers up over my lap and now he set the breakfast table down over it. Seeing it, I picked up a spoon, ready to eat, for I had skipped dinner.

"Have you already eaten this morning?"

He gave me his sideways smile. "Hours ago. Your news stirred up a hornet's nest, and I haven't been to bed at all. Black coffee and toast have kept me going. Do you feel well enough to talk?"

"Of course! I was just a little shocked yesterday. I'm perfectly fine now." Using the back of my spoon, I tapped the shell of the egg in its cup, cracking it to scoop up the goodness inside.

"I am waiting to hear from Lady Talleyrand whether she has been successful in meeting with the king. We will need his approval before agreeing to anything the Brotherhood would want."

"Is His Majesty likely to agree, then?" I had devoured the egg and was now working on buttering a roll before putting on a layer of jam.

"It depends on his mood, which is one of the most difficult things about him. They often coddled the king like a child, and Lady Talleyrand will have to work her magic to get him to come around. Until then, I've put things into motion. Valentina will lunch today with Lady Langenberg so she can pass a message to Mysir Vischeer about a possible meeting."

"Isn't that premature? What if His Majesty does not agree?"

Tristan shrugged. "Lady Talleyrand can use the meeting to learn more about their intentions. Intelligence gathering is always useful."

"Couldn't that be dangerous for her?"

"We will make sure she is well-protected."

As I licked the jam off the corner of my mouth, Tristan stopped talking. I held up my tray, and he took it, setting it aside on a table. Coming back, he sat down on the side of the bed, but while he was physically within reach, his mood seemed distant.

"I'm sorry I wasn't there to protect you."

I shook my head. "Don't be! I wasn't expecting things to turn dangerous."

"You didn't think that yesterday," he pointed out.

"Yesterday, I was not in the best state of mind."

He relaxed. Reaching over my legs, he placed his hand down on the mattress to brace himself as he leaned closer to examine my face. "How does that feel?"

"Sore. I don't think I'll be smiling very much. It hurts to do it!"

His other hand reached over and gently touched my jaw, sweeping down to my chin. I leaned into its caress before he reluctantly pulled away.

"You might end up with a black eye."

I grimaced. "Let's hope not." I didn't want to talk about my face. I wasn't vain, but I didn't want a scar. "Do you think a deal will happen with the Brotherhood? That Vischeer will get what he wants?"

"Uncertain. His Majesty distrusts them. There has always been a tension between the intelligentsia and the royal court. The idea that someone can rise by their own merit, instead of through their bloodline, makes the courtiers uncomfortable. That tension only increased when King Guénard took the throne. As a child he had a sadistic tutor, a horrible, abusive man, and that has made him distrust the institution. It is why he has consistently decreased the university's funding."

"I did not know that was the reason."

"Only his inner circle knows about it, but it is short-sighted. His prejudice has caused Sarnesse harm. Not supporting innovation is why Perino imports twice what we export. It's why we've had to raise the import fees in order to cover our losses."

Guns. My mind immediately went to shiny new guns made by clever people which could shoot across a street to kill someone.

"So you do think Vischeer is right? That someone is using these drugged unfortunates for their own purpose?"

"Oh certainly," said Tristan, nodding. "After the Luminary, I had my agents check the poorest areas of town and the charity hospitals. They confirmed that many of the older patients who were ill or diseased disappeared weeks before. Without a doubt, our master criminal has been sweeping up the desperate to make his little army."

His words made me feel angry and a little sick. How could someone be so callous about human life?

Tristan continued making connections, ticking them off on his fingers one by one. "He returns to the same method: jewels he has stolen or blackmailed away from the rich. Turning that wealth into payments for his henchmen, supplies, and more information to blackmail others. I am sure he has cast quite the wide net. I wonder who is not in his pocket!

"After he returned Lady Talleyrand to her home, De Windt took his men down to the docks and turned it inside out."

"Did he find the weapons?" I asked hopefully.

"No. But he did find bribes, mislabeled boxes, vanished crates, and forged ship manifests. The rot is everywhere." He sighed and slipped sideways to lie on the bed, his hands behind his head. Staring at the ceiling, he mused, "I could just fall asleep here."

Perhaps it was too forward of me, but I replied before I could stop myself, "Why don't you?"

"Too much to do." Still, he didn't seem ready to leave. "Blackmailed jewels to buy guns, and our man pulling all the strings while hiding in the shadows. Which brings us back to Lady Josephine Baudelaire and her necklace. She is slippery and has covered her tracks well. Her husband is a complete idiot who cares only about his hounds and horses. This provides her perfect cover. Married to him, she can go to any society party and mingle with those at the highest level without appearing to be interested in politics at all."

"And befriend the king's mistress," I reminded him.

"Mistress no more. King Guénard sacked her. She's traveling under escort to a winter palace in Zulskaya to practice diplomacy. As she freezes, she'll realize she should never have touched his personal correspondence."

"And Josephine remains free? Why doesn't he deal with her?"

"It surprised no one that he sent off a mistress when he tired of her, but to touch someone from a noble house that high in status? He'll need irrefutable evidence."

How frustrating that we didn't have something more concrete about her! "With her personality, I would think plenty of people would like to gossip about her."

He gave a bitter laugh. "Elinor! No noble is going to admit they are being blackmailed. That's the entire point of blackmail. However, I have discovered a likely line of investigation. Men who took the noble way out of their troubles, or women who disappeared into the country, severing all contact with their city relatives."

"You think they are victims?"

"Possibly. But we need to connect them to what we've found in that safe or other stolen goods. I've got men looking at jewelers in the city who might be involved in fencing stolen goods."

I gasped. *What an idiot I have been.* "My father? Could he—? No, he would never have sold stolen goods," I said firmly. "He was a man of honor. I know he was."

Tristan's eyes were serious, and he took a deep breath before saying, "I wondered when you would make that connection. Considering that he was a favorite with the king and the aristocracy, it is more likely that he discovered something. Knew our mastermind. And met his death because of it."

CHAPTER NINETEEN

After Tristan left, my mind remained too active, thinking over the possibility that there was a connection between my father's murder and the master criminal.

Throwing off the covers, I left my bed to test a theory. Shutting the drapes, I retrieved a candle, brazier, and matches from my bag. After lighting a piece of coal, I dropped some solution into each eye and blinked, letting it change my vision.

Madame Granger had told me my father had transitioned, that he had moved on to the Afterlife. Contrary to what people might think, most of us do this; few linger in the Beyond to become ghosts. Still, after his death, I had wanted to believe there was a way to contact him and spent a few fruitless years trying only to never receive an answer.

Eventually, I agreed Leona was right. He was gone forever. Now, with Twyla's belief he was a guardian, could I find him? Or was the girl just using her fanciful imagination to invent a dramatic story?

At the desk, I set the watch to my left, resting the palm of my hand over the smooth metal of its case. Sprinkling the hot coal with herbs, I stared intently at the burning wick. This was an exercise used by the Morpheus Society to prepare for a séance or a Ghost Talk.

It took longer than usual to settle myself for intrusive thoughts kept invading: what Twyla had said; the unexpected appearance of Sergeant Dupont; and the death of Roux. Again and again, I brought my focus back to my breathing and my heartbeat.

Suddenly, in the blink of an eye, the Beyond opened to my third eye, and the veil between the two worlds thinned.

How to explain the dreamy nothingness of the Beyond? It is a liminal space of between. The twilight when the day has ended, but the night hasn't begun. The space between wakefulness and sleep when you are like a child receptive to the world.

Yet while its foreignness impels our curiosity, it also repels. Like the shiny apple that has corruption at the heart. It exists only as a gateway for souls and if you stay too long, you can become as lost as the ghosts that travel it.

How does a Ghost Talker summon a spirit?

With her heart.

The watch under my hand warmed. The area of my breast with the mark tingled. I held my breath, waiting. Standing on the ledge, wanting so much to hear from him again, I started to hope again. *Is Twyla right?* Was there something here for me?

But then it faded. The watch grew cold. The sensation under my skin faded. There was no answering call. I pulled my mind back, my shoulders slumping. I reached out to extinguish the wick, when something far away caught my ear.

Elinor.

Father?

But it was gone as quickly as it had came. All was silent.

Tristan strongly suggested, in the ways he often suggested things, that I stay put.

Trying to be good, I sent a note to Anne-Marie to bring me a few clothes, as well as some items from my supply cabinet. Upon her arrival, Ruben brought her and my small traveling trunk upstairs. Anne-Marie seemed not to notice his admiring glances as she bustled about my bedroom, arranging things to her satisfaction.

I told him, "That will be all, Ruben. Thank you."

After Tristan's footman left, I asked Anne-Marie, "Did you find the journal I wanted?"

She nodded. Undoing the strap buckles, she opened the trunk and removed a tan leather book from underneath a folded blouse.

"What would you like me to do here, madame?"

"Hm. I don't think there's much. I doubt we will be staying long. Why don't you go downstairs and see if you can bring up a tray for lunch? Tristan and his sister are out for the day, and I really don't want to eat at the table all by myself."

I settled myself in one of the two soft chairs near the window. Whereas my other books were case notes, this journal I used to record my thoughts about my father's murder.

The first entry was from about three months after his death when I was under the guardianship of Leona Granger. This was the day I decided that I would no longer be a victim, but a hunter. The round, schoolgirl handwriting little resembled mine now.

❧

I mean to write down everything before I forget. No matter how I feel, I must remember everything if I'm to bring his killer to justice. Whoever did this shall pay. I will find him no matter what the gendarmes think.

That day started out like any other. I had the same breakfast with Father that I always did at the little table in our kitchen. He drank only coffee, and was not paying attention to my news about the new kittens at the school. Finally, I told him I was going to bring them all home, to which he said nothing! He only nodded.

Distracted (underlined twice).

I left for school at 8:45. It was the last time I saw him alive.

How I wish I had some warning! But no, everything seemed ordinary. Nothing unusual. No mysterious person following me. No feeling of danger. Upper math was as tedious as ever. Everyone was talking about a ship, the Resolute, which had sunk in a tremendous storm the previous weekend. There were no survivors.

I came home at about four. The clock at the bank down the street chimed and I remember thinking it would give me time to make dinner before Father finished his work for the day.

I used my key to enter, discovering the front door to be locked. But I thought it strange the curtains were still closed. The first thing Father always did when taking his mid-morning tea was open the drapes, for he liked to sit there and watch the people walk by.

I called out, but no one answered. The house had an emptiness to it. A quiet that was odd and strange. Or am I adding knowledge in hindsight? I am sure there was a coldness to the air, because I remember my breath forming a cloud in front of my face and wondering if he had forgotten to add fresh coal again.

Was the house waiting for me to find him?

Washed breakfast dishes sat on the drain rack. We were between servants as our last, Nonnie, had left to have her baby. The woman sent by the agency to replace her had quit the day before. What was her name? Brigitta. Last name? Find out. Ask the agency. Penciled in later beside this was the name Meijer.

The kitchen was clean, but as I told the guardia, Father could not abide a mess. He always tidied up things. So did he have lunch? I was not sure.

On the next page was a diagram of the ground floor of our house and his workshop. I had even sketched the location of all the furniture.

At the end of the hall was the door to his workshop. This door was closed but unlocked. Father did not lock it during the day when he was working, although if he was to be gone for any length of time from it, he would.

My hand on the knob, cold in my hand.

I shuddered. Even after all these years, thinking of the before and after affected me.

I must think of what I saw. Father on the floor, on his stomach, the angle of his neck strange. He was dead. There was no doubt of it.

The room had a black floorcloth so he could easily find anything he dropped and to stop anything small falling between the floorboards. It now was brownish red. Blood changes color. Underlined. *What shade?* Underlined twice. *Dark. Not fresh.*

I did not scream. I don't think I could have. My chest froze with no air to draw a breath. It was like one of those nightmares you can't wake up from. Not real, yet terrifying. Finally, I shook off my trance and looked around the room. There was no one else.

The back window was broken. Smashed. Glass shards from it lay on the top of his workbench and on the floor.

He must have been in the middle of working on something, for there were metal shavings on his bench, as well as two of his tools. The stool he used was overturned on the floor next to him.

Under this information was a crude sketch of the position of Father's body and the stool. He was attacked from behind. The only entrance was the door through which I had entered. There was no way that he would not have seen who had come in, so he must not have suspected any act of violence. Or the person had been in the room, hiding. Perhaps in the corner, beside the tall cupboard on that wall?

Was Father in the room when his killer entered? Or did he arrive to find him crawling through the window? Did he surprise a burglar? Was Father killed because someone wanted his precious hoard of stones, the jewelry he was designing or repairing?

The safe was ajar. Papers were on the floor, but I did not see the storage boxes he used for his gemstones and gold. The bookshelf where his ledgers would sit had fallen off the wall, and the scattered books were soaking up his blood.

Looking down, I saw that the toe on one of my boots was becoming red from his blood. I screamed and ran out the door.

I closed my eyes a moment, trying to clear my mind, but all I kept seeing was the blood.

CHAPTER TWENTY

S creaming, I flew out of the house, running to the corner
where there was a fire box alarm. I remember thinking that
I would use it and get help. But on the way, I slammed into
the back of a guardia, walking his beat.

It was Inspector Marcellus Barbier, then a beat officer, before
he rose through the ranks. He took me back and later sat with me
until the station sent someone over more senior to deal with the
severity of the crime. At the end of the day, they gave me to a
neighbor, an old woman who fed the neighborhood cats. She tried
to get me to eat something. I would stay with her for several
months, missing school, listless, refusing to go back into our old
house.

The journal did not have her name. When I returned after my
training, I learned she had moved away to stay with relatives. The
chance to thank her for her kindness was another thing lost among
all the rest.

I started haunting the guardia station, wanting answers.
Wanting action. Everyone knew my name and I could see they
pitied me, especially as the investigation met one dead end after
another. They believed that someone broke in to steal and had

surprised my father. They had killed him before fleeing with the stones and the precious gold and silver bars from the safe he had opened due to working that day.

The journal said it was six months later when Barbier finally took me to meet Leona. After speaking with him at Devereaux's, I guessed he had probably thought Leona would do a séance to reassure me that my father was in a better place. It was what people usually expected from Ghost Talkers.

He saw me a few more times, but our relationship only became a friendship when I sought him out again as an adult. At first he had laughed at my offer of using my Ghost Talking skills to aid the gendarmes in solving crimes. But after a few successes, he finally became convinced I could be useful. Barbier introduced me to Charlotte, and the two of us found we had the same sense of the world, which formed a deeper friendship.

Between them both, I found a calling. Yet as the years passed, I continued on my own the investigation into my father's murder, only to remain stymied at every turn.

My father had been involved in deeper matters than I had thought. This was no simple burglary; it was a crime with ties to people in high places, and to a criminal network that spread throughout Alenbonné.

The only question in my mind was if my father had been a part of it. Or had he stumbled upon these villains and had been silenced by them?

Of course, I had told Tristan that my father was innocent. That was the child in me who wanted to believe in his goodness, but many years had passed since I knew the man, and then I had only known him as a favored daughter.

What had he really been like? His loves and hates? What had he thought of the nobles that he had made lovely things for, but who now sneered at the thought his daughter might marry a man of their set?

And I had also changed. Working to solve crimes with Barbier,

I had seen family members turn against each other and commit horrible crimes, all for the sake of greed or passion.

Today, what was more important to me than who had killed him was to know the truth of the type of man he had been.

Putting my hat on, I opened the bedroom door to leave only to discover Tristan, his hand raised up to knock.

"Tristan!"

"Elinor," he returned. "I met Anne-Marie in the hall. She said you hadn't eaten. I was about to invite you downstairs for lunch." He held out his arm, and I naturally took it.

"Weren't you going to be busy all day?"

"I'm waiting for reports to come in." Looking down, he said with a slow smile, "Do you always eat lunch with your Ghost Talking case with you?"

Wondering if he would be angry, I admitted, "I was going to run an errand when you arrived."

"I will accompany you. After you get something to eat."

He must have told the servants his intention, for the dining room had two place settings. He pulled out a chair for me next to the end of the table and then took the one at the head.

Bread rolls arrived with butter, olives, and sliced peaches. The smell made me suddenly realize I was starving. The butter I spread on the warm bread melted, dripping down my fingers. A servant placed bowls of tomato chickpea soup in front of us.

"Valentina just returned from meeting Lady Langenberg."

"Oh!" I exclaimed with quickening interest. Maybe it was the good food that was starting to make me feel alive again. "What happened?"

"They've decided to host a party."

"Party?" I sagged. What about the Brotherhood? Averting a rebellion? Saving Sarnesse from ruin?

Tristan laid down his spoon and wiped his napkin across his smirk. "Elinor, our brotherly friends cannot officially meet with our government. That would lend their group legitimacy. If it was a sanctioned meeting, then the two parties could not deny that it ever took place or conceal the topics discussed. Meeting in a social setting provides plausible deniability for them both."

"I see." I would never get the hang of political machinations. Just meet and say what you want to say. Why couldn't people be straightforward? It all sounded very confusing and convoluted.

"Valentina will expect you to attend."

"Of course," I agreed mechanically. It seemed wrong to think of parties right now. Our fish entrée arrived. It would be the only meat since it was a luncheon meal.

"Now, tell me what you have been doing today." Tristan must have sensed something was wrong, for he asked gently. "What is this errand you wished to run?"

Perhaps it was for the best that he was here. I would have gone alone and probably ended up stranded or arrested for loitering. "I need to visit my father's old workshop. With this new information we have, perhaps I will find something I've overlooked before."

"We had best have some dessert before we go, do you not think? For sustenance."

After my father's death, the house had become mine. As I was underage and female, the bank had held the deed in trust, renting out the residence. At my request, the workshop was closed and not available for the tenants' use. From the relief the bankers showed, the tenant seemed pleased not to have access to a murder room.

I had visited a few times, attempting to locate clues, but had never found anything significant that would have pointed to his killer. My last visit had been over five years ago, for it was not a place I liked to linger.

In the trade street most of the buildings were for commerce, although some had living accommodations such as ours. While it was late in the afternoon, that still didn't explain the lack of traffic on the street. There should have been shoppers and open stores.

My father's house was at the end of a street on a corner. The driver parked where I indicated and before Tristan could help me out, I opened the door and stepped down. My eyes automatically went to where my father's shop sign should have hung. The board swinging over our heads declared that the storefront was now a tobacconist shop.

"I have a key to the back door so we can get in without disturbing the tenants," I told Tristan as I started towards the gate. Its creaking announced my arrival, and as we entered the yard, a hand drew back a white lace curtain on the upper window. I waved, but the head ducked backward, the drape falling to cover the glass once more. This didn't surprise me. Few wanted anything to do with anyone connected to a violent death.

As I inserted the key into the lock, I found the wooden door had swelled. It took the force of my shoulder to get it to release from the casement.

I'm home, Father.

There was a stillness in the silence, but an absence of life. Only memories haunted the place, not my father. To the left, I reached for the knob to turn on the gas and opened the little box on the wall that held matches to light it. This connected to the main house, and I covered that utility bill every month for both the house and the workshop. It was one of the renters' perks.

The lit gas showed what had once been the old laundry. It was here that I had partitioned the long hall, making a private entrance.

I paused in opening the door, taking a deep breath before swinging it open to fully reveal my father's old workshop. It was dim because the only window was boarded up, so I fumbled with the switch to turn up the gas sconces and lit another match.

It all seemed very far away, small even. Like I was looking down a long tunnel. The old scarred work bench; the stool returned to its usual place under the counter; and his ledgers stacked in the corner. The safe was open and vacant. We had long ago removed anything of importance.

I went over to the workbench to examine it, running my hand over the scars in the wood made by his hammering. There was nothing there except tools for punching, squeezing, and hammering that had created delicate pieces of jewelry. No mysterious diamonds caught in the cracks of the wood. No carved message in the worn wood naming the killer. It was all achingly ordinary and seen many times before.

"This is where it happened," I said, my voice breaking the silence of dust motes.

Tristan was prowling the room, looking for anything that might catch his eye. "Have you checked behind the safe?"

"I would think the gendarmes did, but I didn't. It's too heavy to move on my own."

"Let's try together. Perhaps something fell behind or rolled under it."

Together we pushed it askew, revealing only a dead mouse. I stared down at its desiccated husk. But Tristan had moved on. "What are these?" He picked up one of Father's ledgers from the stack on the floor.

"It holds his diagrams of pieces he was working on, or sketches he planned on designing. I've looked through them before, but I saw nothing that pertained to his death."

He placed the ledger on the workbench and started slowly flipping through the pages. His finger ran down the length of each page as he examined it. "Your father made beautiful things."

I came to look over his shoulder to see that he was viewing a drawing of a necklace. It was made from silver shaped into leaves, with pearls serving berries. "That one included a matching tiara and earrings. He designed it for a winter bride."

Another page revealed the sketch of a delicate filigree earring set. "That one was gold with opals."

"You remember them?"

"Most of them. And even if I didn't, Father made notes on each page." I pointed to the measurements next to numbers and the line of letters at the bottom.

"I don't see that it says opals here."

"He had a shorthand." My finger ran along the notation. "The letter C means it was a commission and not one he had made to sell. Here is the grade of gold. The OP means the stone he used was opals. The R next to OP means the person commissioning the piece supplied the stones."

"Are all the diagrams identified like this?"

"Oh yes. He was very meticulous in his work. I used to tease him about it by calling him Grandfather because he was so fussy about how everything was so well organized." I reached over and, taking control of the book, thumbed through the diagrams of rings, earrings, cuff links, and necklaces until I found the one I wanted. "This was my favorite as a child, but he thought it too fanciful."

It was a necklace, with the central piece being the body of a fairy woman. Her outspread arms wrapped around the wearer's throat, and she wore a flowing dress studded with diamonds. The toes of her bare feet would have pointed down, drawing the eye to a woman's cleavage.

My eyes wandered to the bottom of the page, to the stain of dark brown. Old blood. I slammed it shut.

"Would you mind if we took these books back with us?"

"Not at all. If you think they could help."

Tristan's eyes gleamed with interest, like a cat in the dark staring at a mouse-hole. "What I'm thinking is that we could match some of these descriptions to the stolen goods we've found. Or find out if there is a link to the nobles I believe were victims. I think your father's books are probably the closest we have to a comprehensive list of valuables owned by the aristocracy. Other than the inventory he did of King Guénard's collection."

I nodded in agreement. "He did do a lot of work for nobles. It is why he gave up the public shop and met clients only by appointment."

He tapped the book. "Do you think the Baudelaire necklace would be in here?"

I frowned, concentrating. "I don't remember it, but I haven't looked through them since meeting her. Of course, it would have been in her husband's family at the time."

"True." He started picking up the other volumes and stacking them on the workbench. "Are these all about his work?"

"Yes. I think so. It's been some time since I've looked through them all. The ledger listing that year's client accounts was missing at the time of his death. I remember it driving the bank wild, as they did not know who could make a claim for any stolen jewelry in his possession. In the end they had to rely upon my memory of what I'd seen in the safe before the burglary."

Tristan looked around the workroom. "Did he keep an appointment book?"

I sighed. "Also missing."

"You're too close, Elinor, or you'd have seen it. Whoever did this was a client. Or related to a client. They couldn't afford their appointment being found and their relationship to your father being made."

I blinked. "I don't see—? The gendarmes thought they took the client list so they could commit other burglaries at houses of the well-to-do."

"And was there a rash of burglaries like that afterward?"

"Yes, there had been a few. I remember them being in the paper."

"The appointment book being missing removes the possibility of this being a random act; some casual burglar breaking in, knowing this was a jeweler's place of business and who hoped to score. It narrows the field of suspects. It won't be the grocer or a housemaid, but someone who had work done with your father. Not someone regularly seen here, but someone new."

"Why a new client?"

"Because you, or someone else in society, would have recalled an old business relationship. Gossip runs like water downhill."

"So the answer could be in there." My eyes traveled to the tower of ledgers Tristan had made from my father's notebooks. He followed my gaze. "Yes."

CHAPTER TWENTY-ONE

"I came here thinking— Oh, never mind. Thank you for thinking of the ledgers," I told him and turned toward the door.

Tristan grabbed my upper arm, stopping me. "If it wasn't the books you wanted, what did you think to find?"

I shook my head. "Twyla told me last night something that made me wonder if I came back here, would I feel his presence?"

"When did you meet her?" he asked, puzzled. "No one told me she had come to the house."

Holding out my hands, palms up, I said, "She didn't. I know this may sound wild, but I met her in my dreams."

He showed surprise, but recovered well. "Who knows what that girl will do next? What did she say?"

"That my father is a guardian looking after me."

Tristan frowned, puzzled. "Guardian? Is that a special type of spirit?"

I sighed. "There is a rumor among the spiritualists that there are beings from the highest plane, the Afterlife, who try to guide our life here. That they provide signs to us that help us make better choices. Not to get on the train that gets derailed. To go to a party where you meet your soulmate. Things of that nature. However, there is no hard proof that such exists! It's utter nonsense, of course. My father isn't here. I don't feel him at all."

Tristan searched my face. To avoid his gaze, I ended up looking down at my hands. He mused out loud, "You said that rather forcibly. It's been my experience that the more someone is adamant about something they say can't be, the more it is. Are you sure you don't feel him?"

How frustrating to be in love with a man who was a professional interrogator! It would be so much easier if he accepted things one said at face value, even if they were lies or half-truths.

"I'm not sure. Exactly," I said, hedging.

"Tell me what makes you unsure."

"It sounds silly," I protested, but his hand gestured for me to continue. "Remember when I first met you and you made me wait in an office at the gendarmes?" He nodded. "Well, I was so tired, I fell into a doze. I dreamed my father spoke to me about rubies made from dragon's blood. Then, of course, the dragon happened. Which all seems too much of a coincidence, don't you think?"

"Hm. Any other incidents like that?"

At least he hadn't said I was a fool!

"Marcus found my father's old pocket watch in a pawnshop. It went missing then. Presumably stolen. When the boy returned it to me, it left a mark on my skin." I indicated where by laying my hand over my breast. "It's not a physical mark— Leona called it a psychic burn. Only a few see it. Charlotte and Anne-Marie cannot, but Twyla and Leona Granger can. And you."

He stepped closer, his hand coming up to lie over where mine rested. Concerned, he asked, "This? Does it hurt?"

"Sometimes. When Frida Korver, one of the dead girls, left me at the theater to remove the souls of the Ghastlys, it hurt a lot. Again when Meike left to take Dupont with her. Other times it just grows warm."

Putting his arm around my shoulders, he said, "You've never said anything about this to me."

Of course not! It was an anomaly I didn't understand, so I wasn't comfortable with even thinking about it. "When I talked to Leona about it, she said if I ignored it, it would fade away."

"But it hasn't?" I shook my head, and he wrapped me in his arms, his chin dislodging my hat to rest on my forehead. "Why are you frightened?"

"I'm not. If this is my father speaking to me from the Afterlife, shouldn't I take comfort in that?"

"But you don't, do you? I can hear it in your voice that you don't."

Floundering, I compromised. "I'm just uncomfortable with it."

Tristan gave a chuckle, and I could feel the vibration of it in his chest where both my hands lay. "The woman who talks to ghosts and defeats dragons is uncomfortable with her father returning from the dead so he can give her advice?"

I broke away from his hold to chastise him. "I'm serious, Tristan! This is unprecedented. If he's back from the Afterlife, what does that mean for how we view our souls and what happens to them? What if this leads to the living gaining access to the Afterlife? Parnell has shown us how horrible things are when you meddle with the natural order of death. What if someone tried something similar in the Afterlife?"

Tristan put his hand on my shoulder, giving it a squeeze. "You are seeing monsters under the bed, my dear. You don't have an open invitation to the Afterlife. Neither has he spoken with you and revealed secrets about it. Don't get ahead of yourself." He paused and then added sternly, "Unless there is something else you aren't telling me?"

"No. I told you everything. But the Morpheus Society said that no one returns from the Afterlife. It's a one-way journey!"

He laid a finger over my lips. "May I remind you that Twyla

shouldn't be able to move her physical body into the Beyond, but she does? The Morpheus Society is no more all-knowing than any organization that explores what we don't understand. Look at science. Did you ever dream of anything like electricity existing before a decade ago? There are those who break ground so others can follow."

"Lady Alouette Sarte," I said, naming the founder of the Morpheus Society.

"And you may be the next who leads them forward into some new research, some new understanding."

I shook my head. "I don't think so. That will be Twyla."

"Stop comparing yourself to her. I don't discount that the girl has unusual talents but sometimes hard work will triumph over natural skill. And surely brains will triumph over silliness. She has a long way to go before she will match you." He paused for a moment, his eyes examining me. "Have you ever thought you might have outgrown the Morpheus Society, Elinor?"

"No. Not really. But I think they feel I have outgrown them." I told him what Leona and Twyla had said about the faction at the Society which wanted me out. "It's only politics. It will blow over once things calm down."

He looked skeptical. "Sometimes things fade away when the next scandal arises, but it's been my personal experience that some mud sticks. I don't like this, Elinor. It seems they want you to blame for their own dirty dealings with Parnell. What would happen if they forced you out? Would that stop you from being able to do your Ghost Talking?"

"No," I said slowly, feeling worried. "I don't see how that could happen. The Morpheus Society is only an organization, not a legal body. They don't control my abilities, if I can practice, or if I solicit clients. What would be a bother is losing the credentials of being a member of such a prestigious organization. Not being able to access their research or resources. Also, having my work sanctioned by them does give me a certain authenticity that a freelancer, like Madame Nyght, lacks."

"Madame Nyght had a thriving clientèle," pointed out Tristan.

I laughed for the first time that evening. "Yes, but that put her in jail in the end, remember?"

"She was a fraud. You aren't. Also, she didn't have me in her pocket." He gave me a quick kiss. "It all depends on which side of the law you are on if you ended up behind bars."

"So I need to be sure to keep you sweet, do I?"

"Definitely."

By the time we exited, the sun was starting to set. It was past midsummer and even now, the evening daylight hours were becoming shorter.

"Damn the man."

"What? Is something wrong?" My back was to Tristan as I locked the back door.

"My driver. He must be walking the horses to keep them from fretting. Stay here while I check down the block and see if I can find him." He put the stack of journals by the inside of the gate and, exiting, turned right. "Stay there!"

"I will!" I called back.

After he left, I walked around the yard, noticing that the tenant had put in a small vegetable garden, which was weedy and needed watering. The outdoor pump still worked, and I took one of my gloves off to catch some water to wet my lips. How many times had I done the same as a child?

Settling the handle down so it wouldn't leak, I was pulling back on my glove when I felt a shiver run down my spine. My hand went to my pocket, as a voice from the gate called my name.

"Madame Chalamet." It was Sergeant Dupont. Or what was animating his body.

I hoped my pause in speaking wasn't too long to appear suspicious. "Sergeant. Is Inspector Barbier about?" I asked, trying to express myself as innocently as possible.

"No. Only me."

Tristan had latched the gate upon his exit, but the padlock and its chain dangled to the side. Nothing would prevent him from entering the yard. I moved a little closer, hoping that the closed distance would prevent him from opening the gate. It was not so close he could grab me.

"Are you working here about? I imagine you are staying busy with the unrest in the city."

"Very busy." Why did his answer sound sly? Or had he always talked this way, and I had been too stupid to notice?

Hurry, Tristan!

Trying to sound chatty, I told him, "I was only checking on my tenant. This was my father's house back in the day, and now it is mine."

"I know." Dupont had not worked on my father's case. How would he know this place meant anything to me? I didn't ask. That would take me into dangerous territory. Things were already perilous.

"A friend of mine thought he saw you in the student quarter. Do you live thereabouts?"

He nodded slowly. I watched in horrified anticipation as his hand came up on the iron bars of the gate, sliding down their length to the latch handle. I said hastily, trying to stop that hand moving, "What do you think of the riots? It doesn't seem safe to be on the streets."

The gate creaked, and he stepped into the yard. A shiver ran up my arms. I was not a tall woman, and Dupont was a big man. He was also unnatural. Removed from his soul, it was doubtful that whatever was animating him would have a moral compass or restraint.

"It isn't safe. Outside or inside. Downtown or uptown. Above ground or below."

The street was quiet. No one about. No one to hear a shout for help, even if I could scream loud enough. I swallowed, trying to wet my mouth. The yard wasn't a big lot, and there was no possibility of evading him, only of delaying the inevitable. Or to scare him away. Unlikely, but I tried. "I'm waiting on my friend. You remember him. The Duke de Archambeau?"

"He's gone. Chasing his horses that took a fright." I did not like his smile. It seemed a bit too like that of Vonn, the killer of girls.

Moving to the right, increasing the distance between us, I said, "There is one thing I would like to know." *There were a million!* "Did you kill Parnell? Because that broken neck at the base of the stairs seemed a little too convenient."

"Crack-crack," he gloated.

"What about Hannah Wahl, Ebby Losendahl's maid?"

"Vonn killed her," he said, putting his hands together in mock prayer, and looking to the sky. He walked slowly towards me, knowing I had little space to maneuver away from him. There was no way for me to reach the gate before him.

"But it wasn't Vonn who beat her and dumped her in that alley, was it? That was you, I think. Why?"

Dupont giggled. It was high-pitched, so odd coming from a man of his size that it frightened me more than this relentless circling of me. He had edged me into a corner despite my best effort to reach the gate. "I was told to get rid of her. Like Parnell. They both talked too much. Like you."

"Who told you to do that?"

"Talk, talk, talk. Stop talking."

His hands came up to wrap around my neck, choking me. I fell against him, pressing closer. Bringing my hand over his heart, I shot him with the palm-sized pistol I had concealed in my hand.

Chapter Twenty-Two

D upont's fingers dug into my neck, choking me. I fired the second round, my last, the recoiling gun bruising my hand.

He slumped against me, the dead weight pushing me to the ground. On my knees, I shoved him away. Hitting the ground, he rolled onto his back, gasping. A pool of blood spreading across his shirt front reminded me of how Roux had died.

A swirling black-gray smoke rose from his body as life faded from Dupont. The vapor coalesced, becoming denser. Instinctively, I raised the gun, even though it was useless.

In the street, the duke's carriage pulled up to the curb. Sitting next to the driver was Tristan.

"Don't come any closer!" I shouted at him, but of course, that only made him leap down from the box seat and rush to the gate. There he hesitated, taking in the scene of Dupont's prone body and the dark cloud of evil.

"What is that?" He said in a quiet voice.

"Whatever was animating Sergeant Dupont," I told him, never taking my eyes off it. The oily smoke swirled faster, getting denser as the body grew colder. I leaned back, my mind horrified as it twitched, and started to redirect itself in my direction.

But other aid rose to help me. My two soul-sisters, who could do nothing against the living, now took charge. Their auras materialized and formed a gold dome over me.

The thing flung itself at me with the ferocity of a rabid dog. For a moment, I gained an impression of its depraved desires, impotent rage, and hideous pleasures, before the gold shield threw it back.

It screamed, its tendrils of black vapor clawing to reach me. The gold light shaped itself into the form of Louisa Bonnet. She set my heart aside with tender care and then she was gone. Our bond dissolved like water slipping through my hands. She was so gentle I could have cried.

Her harp did not try to drown out the ranting screams of the thing. Instead, it brought the raucous sounds into her melody and forced them to dance to her tune.

Across the yard, Tristan made the mistake of opening the gate. Immediately, Dupont's soul-shadow pulled back from me, trying to escape Louisa it shot towards Tristan.

"Stay back! Please, stop!" I cried out. Tristan froze as one black tendril of the thing extended like the arm of an octopus, coming closer. From across the yard I met his shocked eyes. Once he had experienced a possession by a lovelorn scholar, but not anything this evil.

"Help him!" I begged Louisa Bonnet.

She was already moving. Her gold-sculpted arms elongated, wrapping around all of Dupont's shadow. Drawing it back to her, she became a glass bottle enclosing the shadow, sealing it away. Contained, it swirled violently, trying to find an escape.

The gold became less transparent, concealing it from view. Louisa's body grew taller, more cylindrical. Like the two girls before, the gold shot up to the sky like a shaft of light. In a heartbeat, it burst and was gone, leaving behind only a scattering of gold motes floating around us.

"Elinor!" Tristan was at my side, his arm around me.

"Dupont. He found me." My voice was hoarse, my throat swollen and bruised.

Tristan didn't look at the body that lay on the ground. Instead, he gently took away the gun hanging loosely from my hand.

"Anne-Marie will never get my gloves clean. I will have to throw them away." I started to cry seeing the powder burns.

"Can you tell me what happened? Was that gold thing one of the dead girls?" asked Tristan, wiping away my tears.

"Yes, that was Louisa Bonnet. She saved us from being possessed by that horrible thing! He wasn't a Ghastly. That's why his body isn't a pile of bones and skin. Something cut Dupont's soul from it and then took possession of it."

"Come here. Let me get you into the coach."

He kept his body between mine and the one on the ground as he held me against his side. Trying not to stumble, I asked, "Where was your driver?"

"He took the horses for a drive around the block. Some street kids down the block were banging on storage drums with sticks and they were fretting."

"I think Dupont planned that."

He opened the door and lifted me up to the seat. "Rest here and let me see to everything."

I leaned my head against the interior, telling him, "Be careful. Don't touch it!"

Tristan squeezed my hand hard. "I'm sorry I wasn't here to help you. Again."

"Next time I'll let you save me." I tried to smile and failed. "You did tell me to keep my gun with me all the time."

"I'm thankful that there was one piece of my advice you listened to. Now wait here."

As he left, I gave a heavy sigh. Louisa Bonnet had left me far more gently than my other two soul sisters, but I felt drained of all energy. Limp. Distantly, in some remote part of my mind, I felt pity for poor Sergeant Dupont. Not for the thing that had worn his body like an old coat, but for the man he had been. The man I had never got to know.

Tristan returned with the stack of my father's journals and put them beside me on the seat. "I am going to send you home."

"You aren't coming?" I asked, feeling a tremor of fear run through me. What if something else happened?

"My dear, I cannot leave him here. People will need to be told. Questions answered."

"Oh, yes. Sorry. Of course you do. Your duty would require that."

"Are you afraid?"

"Yes."

"Stay here."

I wasn't sure where I would go, but I nodded anyway. He moved out of sight to the front of the coach, where I heard him talking to his driver. "Get down, I'll take the horses. You will stay with the body until I return."

"But, Your Grace, that thing! What was it? You can't leave me here!"

"I certainly can! You should have thought of us when you decided to take my horses off for a tour of the neighborhood!"

There was a jerk of the carriage beneath me, and I craned my neck to see Tristan pull Davis down from his perch. Tristan climbed up and took the reins. He opened a storage box under the driver's seat.

"Now, to make you feel better, here's my brace of pistols. You take one and I'll keep the other. I'll return with the gendarmes after."

The horses bolted forward, and I had to grab my father's ledgers to stop them from falling to the ground. It seemed we all wanted to be away from such a thing.

We reached Hartwood in the middle of dinner. It was the second time I had arrived with another man's blood on me.

"Tristan! What has happened?" Valentina rose from the table, her eyes wide with surprise and concern.

Around the table sat Lady Maryegold Talleyrand, Lady Tulip Langenberg, and Mysir Sven de Windt. The last had a forkful of food that had frozen halfway to his mouth upon our entrance.

"We are fine, Valentina. However, I shall be taking de Windt with me, which will sadly disorder your party, I'm afraid. We have a situation." In response, de Windt hastily put his fork down and pushed back his chair. "After a change of clothes, I'm sure Madame Chalamet would be glad to join you."

With that, Tristan gave a bow and left me behind. I wasn't sure if I wouldn't have preferred to be with him and de Windt than a party of such noble ladies. To Lady Talleyrand, Tulip, and Valentina, I said, "Please don't let me interrupt you. I'll go upstairs and get changed."

Valentina was still standing, napkin in hand. With her brother gone, she demanded, "What has happened?"

"I will tell you about it when I return. Right now, I'd like to get into fresh clothes."

She nodded reluctantly. Lady Tulip left her seat and came to stand beside me. "Why don't you entertain Lady Talleyrand as I help Elinor? We will return quickly."

We went up the stairs without a word. I was trying to compile my thoughts into some sort of story. How much to say, and what not to say. The young woman beside me only gave me curious looks.

Upon entering my room, we found Anne-Marie. She jumped up from where she had been sitting, dropping her darning to the floor in surprise. "Madame!"

I raised a hand to stop any further outcry. "I know, I know. But it isn't my blood. Now I need out of these clothes and into some-thing clean."

"Something appropriate for dinner," Lady Tulip explained.

I really didn't need two women fussing over me, but I have to admit it did get me ready much faster. The blood had soaked through my blouse to stain my skin. With some washing up and new clothes, no one would have guessed I had shot Sergeant Dupont to death.

"Keep the clothes, Anne-Marie. I don't know if they are evidence or not."

Neither of the two women said anything to my statement, only shared a silent look.

In fresh clothes, we left. Outside in the hall, Lady Tulip stopped me. "Elinor, do you trust Lady Talleyrand?"

"I trust no one. Well, obviously except for Anne-Marie and Tristan."

As we descended the stairs, she asked in a low voice, "What I mean is, do you think she is speaking in good faith when she asks for this meeting with the Brotherhood?"

"Ah." My mind had been dwelling on personal matters like the murder of my father, body-snatching, and shooting a guardia. I had forgotten about the sorry state of the kingdom. "Like anything political, I think she may mean well. Naturally, though, her inter-ests will align with His Majesty's point of view. I would agree to the meeting, but as my friend Jacques would say, keep your powder dry."

When we returned to the dining hall, they were finishing the meat course. Still, Valentina ordered the footman to bring the first course for me. "We shall stay until you have some sustenance, Elinor."

"Thank you." De Windt's place was gone as if he had never sat down to dinner and someone whisked a new plate setting in front of me.

Over the next half hour, I could see that Valentina was struggling with the urge to pepper me with a half a dozen questions. However, that would not do for the perfect hostess. Etiquette required that in-depth personal discussions wait until we adjourned to the sitting room.

She and Lady Talleyrand discussed the latest art exhibition at the Academy. Lady Tulip asked if either of them had heard of a new sports club, which was for ladies only? It provided a very nice lawn court for tennis.

The drone of ordinary talk calmed my mind as I worked my way through soup, fish, and pheasant. None of the three attempted to draw me into conversation, for which I was grateful.

Perhaps I had threatened to do it, but I had never killed a man before. It took some time to digest. While I had no choice, it still was disturbing.

After dinner, we all adjourned. Valentina had the servants distribute coffee and light drinks. When we were behind closed doors, the questions began.

"Elinor, please tell us what happened. Is Tristan safe?"

"I cannot guarantee that he is, but I feel that he will be fine. The danger seems to be past."

"What was the danger?" asked Lady Tulip. She had chosen a glass of sherry, and in her peach colored dress looked much better than the last time I had seen her.

"His Grace had gone with me to visit my father's old workshop. It is in the merchant quarter. There we were attacked by a man who is responsible for the death of Parnell Lafayette of the Morpheus Society and the murder of Hannah Wahl, a maidservant of Lady Ebbe Losendahl."

While I took a sip of my coffee, Lady Valentina explained to the others who I meant. "Lady Ebbe is the daughter of Baron Viktor Losendahl, a dear friend of Tristan's from Zulskaya. Mysir

Lafayette, a member of the Morpheus Society seduced her from the safety of her family. Thankfully, she is now safely back with her parents."

"I remember reading about him in the paper. How many girls had he beguiled?" asked Lady Talleyrand, though Tulip found more interest in the sparkle of her glass than the conversation. I'm sure the talk of seduction by an unscrupulous man smacked too close to home.

"At least five, including Lady Ebbe," I said. "He died of a broken neck from a fall, but the man shot tonight admitted to murdering him. He was not involved directly in the murder of Hannah Wahl, but was an accomplice."

"Shocking," murmured Lady Talleyrand.

"Who was the man?" Lady Tulip asked.

"Sadly, it was a member of the gendarmes. A guardia by the name of Sergeant Dupont. I knew him through my work with Inspector Barbier, but in the last month Dupont had deserted his post. No one could find him." I wasn't sure if I should bring up the circumstances, but decided to do so, as I didn't know when I would meet Lady Tulip again. "I believe he was the one leading the rioters that your friend saw in the student quarter."

Lady Tulip's mouth made an O of surprise.

"I'm sure Tristan had to do what he had to do," said Valentina, concluding erroneously that her brother had shot Dupont. I didn't have the energy to disprove that notion. From Lady Talleyrand's interested gaze upon me, I did not think she had made that mistake. At least she didn't voice her thought to the room.

With the murder discussed, Valentina refilled everyone's glasses and said, "Let us move on to more cheerful subjects." She raised her own glass. "May our party unite our country once more."

Everyone raised their glass and seconded her toast.

CHAPTER TWENTY-THREE

There was much to do, but none of it concerned me. Tristan put me firmly under an order to stay at Hartwood and not interfere.

"I promise if there is any news, I shall tell you immediately," he told me.

"But I could help you!"

"As soon as I have a dead body to deal with, you will be the first one I shall call. Meanwhile, let de Windt and I do what we are best at— questioning suspects and chasing leads." Tristan gave me a kiss like that would soothe my feelings. Instead, I simmered with resentment.

My irritation with him was probably why I let Dr. Devereaux hypnotize me.

⁓

"Do you wish to receive him, madame? If not, I can tell him you are not at home," said Ruben.

The footman had found me reading a book in the Hartwood conservatory. It had been a quiet day, and I was finding myself bored and restless. Tristan was off with de Windt, doing important work, and Valentina was running errands to prepare for her dinner party. She had invited me, but the idea of choosing dinner plate patterns had made me want to run away.

"Did he say what he wanted to see me about?" I asked, closing my book and setting it aside. At last, there was someone new to speak with.

"No. He only presented his card and asked if you were at home receiving visitors." Ruben presented it to me on a little silver tray designed to hold nothing but calling cards. The pomp at Hartwood was all rather ridiculous when you thought about it too much.

"I'll come down and visit with him."

Ruben gave me a little bow and retreated.

"Thank you for agreeing to meet me, Madame Chalamet. I tried calling upon you at the Crown, but when I did not find you there, I asked Dr. LaRue about you and she informed me you were staying here."

With a gesture, I invited him to sit across from me.

"Lady Fontaine invited me to stay for a few days. How are you, Dr. Devereaux? I hope you've recovered from the shock of what happened to Mysir Roux?"

His face did carry hints of a strain. While his skin was naturally pale from spending much of his time indoors, it showed a man who had lost too much sleep, and his large dark eyes were as sorrowful as ever. However, his deep voice still could caress you with its richness.

"I wanted to reassure you it wasn't your fault what happened," he said. "I actually blame myself for Mysir Boutin's— I mean Roux's death. If he had only been truthful about his background, perhaps we could have saved him." He lightly punched his thigh in frustration.

"Put your mind at ease, Dr. Devereaux, I do not blame myself that someone assassinated Roux." Ruben had brought refreshments, and I raised the teapot to inquire, "How do you take your tea?"

"A touch of cream, please. Just a touch." I handed him his cup and started pouring mine. "Have the gendarmes discovered anything more about the situation?"

"The appointment made by your mystery woman was certainly a ruse. Inspector Barbier sent me a note to say that he found the address on her calling card to be as false as the name Boutin was."

"I feared as much," replied Devereaux. "What about the killer? Who fired that shot?"

"I'm afraid they have not discovered that either. His Grace informed me that the shooter used a room in a building across the street. It seems that someone rented it a month ago, shortly after Mysir Roux consulted you. The landlord said the rental was all done by letter and no one saw the person coming or going. The building is mostly empty, as it is undergoing renovations. They found the stand he used for his rifle and spent shot on the floor. Of him, though, there were no clues."

We both sighed, frustrated. Tristan had given me the news before leaving and it had not lifted my mood. We were meeting too many dead ends when all I wanted was action!

"But why would someone want him dead?"

"I'm afraid Mysir Roux cheated some people during an illegal transaction. They did not take it kindly."

"A liar among thieves."

I nodded, sadly. Discussing Roux made me think of his wealth and the promises he had made to the doctor. "Whatever of his legacy, though, to you? Did you go through with his requirements to watch his body and grave?"

Dr. Devereaux's response was vehement. "No. I cannot in all good conscience take it! The man died under my care because I did not take his fears seriously enough."

I clucked in sympathy. *All that money that could have done good, now wasted!* It would probably sit at the bank until the state decided on some way they could take it.

"They traced the drug he took back to the chemist, but the woman denied she gave it to him. A silly lie, and she is sitting in jail now because of it," I told him.

"It acted almost like an anesthesia," said the doctor.

"I do think Mysir Roux had seen others slip into such a coma, which is why he worried they might bury him alive. At least now that won't happen due to the manner of his death."

"It is a small thing to be thankful for," said Devereaux morosely. "Addiction leaves a path of nothing but devastation behind not only for the addict but also for his family. Once it gets a man in its grip, few come out the other side. I have tried hypnotism with a few of them, but it is not always successful in breaking the craving."

Devereaux's comment caught my interest. "Hypnotism? I have used it myself in a small way to help with my Ghost Talk work. I would be very interested in knowing how you use it in your practice."

He chuckled. Now that he was on professional ground, Devereaux's demeanor grew confident and relaxed. He crossed his legs and leaned back against the sofa, the teacup on his knee. "The mind is a far more interesting land of contradictions and wonders than you can imagine. A person grows more suggestible when in a trance state and that is why a mentalist on stage can get them to act out silly behaviors under the command. However, that also gives an opening to influence the mind in other ways. Ways to improve itself."

"Really? How so?" I asked skeptically. "Surely once the person wakes up, they know they are not a chicken and act as they always do."

"Have you ever performed a behavior without thinking of it? Like biting your nails, twirling your hair, or cracking your fingers?"

"A bad habit?"

"Yes. We believe a part of our mind is always responding to the world around us, but the thinking area of the brain is not fully aware of what it is doing. Like your footman here. He brought in tea and cake, but we did not engage him in conversation. We do not know what he thinks, his dislikes and likes. But while this area of the mind serves us, it could do this either well or poorly."

I thought about what he described. "I'm still struggling with this idea. Please continue."

"Maybe you hear some distressing news, and before you realize what you have done, you have eaten the entire tin of biscuits?"

I laughed. "Doesn't everyone do that?"

He smiled. "Well, perhaps we do! The servant mind knows we are upset and gives us what it thinks we need. But do we actually need an entire tin? Could we not have stopped after two or three? Hypnotism lets me talk with the servant and help it understand what the person needs."

"But do these results last?"

He shrugged. "To be honest, they sometimes return. This is a new science, after all. I am just making a suggestion. To make a permanent change, the patient must want it. Not all do want to improve."

"So, is that all you use it for? To remove bad habits?" I set my tea aside, too interested in what he was saying to devote myself to food.

"Yes, and also for clients to find experiences that have held them back for too long. Patients under this treatment are so often so relaxed that they reveal things even they have forgotten. Incidents from their childhood. Interactions with people they would have sworn they had never met if asked when awake. In a trance state, the mind is so relaxed that it finds information that is often concealed from them by the servant mind."

Pondering what he had told me, I suddenly had an idea. "I think there might be a problem you can help me with."

He handed me his cup, and I refilled it. "I will try."

"I am not sure how much Dr. LaRue told you of my history?"

"Only that you had assisted her in many troublesome cases. She gave me a brief survey of your talents as a Ghost Talker."

"What Charlotte did not tell you was *why* I became interested in criminal matters. My father was murdered at home. I wasn't there, but later discovered his body."

He nodded as he listened. I can only imagine how many boxes I was ticking on his list: young and impressionable, sudden trauma, a quest for justice, the death of a parent. To be on the end of being analyzed was uncomfortable. How odd! Was this what my patients sometimes felt when I saw through them?

"Your mother was not alive at the time?"

"No, she died of an illness some years before this happened. When I was nine, she and my younger brother passed away due to the city cough. My father raised me."

"How long ago was your father's murder?"

"Almost thirteen years ago, when I was seventeen."

Our conversation lapsed as he waited for me to proceed. When I did not, he enquired softly, "Has something happened recently to upset you about this sad event?"

I cleared my throat, which was still sore from Dupont's attack. "Yes. I have received some reliable information that my father has returned."

"That he wasn't dead?"

"I'm sorry, I'm making a muddle of this. It's not uncommon for someone who died a violent death, or who met a sudden end, to produce a ghost. At the time though, I was told his soul had moved on to the Afterlife."

"Being a Ghost Talker, that information must have been devastating."

This conversation is getting more convoluted than ever! I needed to explain everything from the beginning. "I'm sorry, I am telling this all backwards."

Devereaux gave a soft little chuckle. "Do not worry about that, Madame Chalamet. It is often the case when I first meet with someone. Usually by the time people come to me, the problem they are seeking help for has reached quite a tangled state. This is normal. Proceed whenever you are ready."

The doctor was quite good at making one feel at ease. "It's good to know that I'm falling into a common pattern."

"Why would that reassure you?"

"It means you will have the experience to help me."

He laughed. "You are an unusual woman, madame."

"Please, just Elinor. I would like to explain what happened in sequence and then what I need help with." He nodded in agreement, encouraging me to proceed.

"Because of my mother's death, my father did put me in school. It was not a boarding arrangement, and I came home every day to stay the night with him. He was a jeweler and his workshop was also our home. One afternoon, I came home to find him dead. Murdered. The investigator thought at the time that he had interrupted someone burglarizing his store of precious gemstones.

"I had no living relatives, so everyone was quite puzzled about what to do about me. Especially as I was not dealing well with the way my father had died. Eventually, Inspector Barbier— well, he was only a street officer then— took me to a Ghost Talker. Madame Leona Granger. I don't expect you have heard of her?"

He shook his head. "Until you, I have never had dealings with any of your profession."

"Well, she was quite high in the Morpheus Society. Even now. So she took me on as an apprentice."

The dark eyes examined me. "Why?"

"What do you mean?" I asked, puzzled at having my narration interrupted.

"Why take in an orphaned girl she had not met before? I assume you had had no relationship before?"

"No. We had not." I thought over his question and started speaking slowly. "I think she felt sorry for me. She often took in young girls as apprentices. It's part of the mentoring system of training the Morpheus Society provides to any interested in pursuing the profession."

"But if she was high up, why did she have to do that? Wouldn't she have reserved her patronage for the wealthy and powerful? Were there other apprentices during your time there?"

"No." This had nothing to do with what I wanted to discuss. "Anyway, when I was with her Leona tried to reach my father and that is when I discovered he was not a ghost but had transcended to the Afterlife."

"Something has happened that throws this into doubt for you." He did not ask this as a question, but stated it as fact. Still, I nodded.

"My apprentice, well, now she is Leona's apprentice, has told me that my father is here on this plane." I told him briefly about the experiences I'd had that made me think he had tried to send me messages.

"Fascinating. This precognitive ability you speak of, you have not had it before?"

"The first episode was when I was in a dream-state. This is a common time for spirits to communicate with the living, but I have never seen the future until I dreamed of my father mentioning rubies and dragons."

He set his cup down on the table beside him and leaned forward. "I'm afraid this is well beyond my experience, Elinor. The supernatural is not my realm. Perhaps you should consult with others in the Morpheus Society?"

I vehemently shook my head. "No. That is out of the question. However, you have made me think there could be another way."

"What way?"

"I believe something inside of me is stopping me from communicating with him. Whenever I think of my father and almost make a connection, something closes me off."

I put my teacup back on its saucer and set them both on the table. Meeting his eyes, I said, "I want you to hypnotize me and break down that wall."

CHAPTER TWENTY-FOUR

Being hypnotized was almost too easy.

Devereaux stood up, and going to the windows in the room, he unhooked the drapery ties, and let them fall. With the room dimmer, he returned to sit beside me. Picking up a clean spoon from the tea cart, he showed it to me.

"I usually use a candle or watch, but I did not come prepared, so we will try this."

"A spoon?"

"It's shiny and draws the eye. Look upon it while we talk. You may grow sleepy, your lids barely able to keep open. That is fine. There is nothing to fear about the hypnosis. It is only a tool to help you relax. Your eyes grow heavy. Consider it like a waking dream."

"Mm-hm," I muttered, not quite convinced. I almost told him to wait until Tristan was home, but that would sound silly, so I did not. I was in his house and well protected. Besides, I didn't know when he would return. After all, Tristan didn't think he needed me on his investigations and so why did I need him involved with mine? All I had to fear were memories.

"There is no hurry. Just focus on the spoon while you tell me more about this block that you wish to remove." Deveraux's pose was comfortably relaxed. With his hand on his shorter arm, he started toying with the spoon handle, twisting it that way and this.

"I've tried using a séance, but each time, my mind hits a wall."

"How does this wall manifest itself? Do you feel it? See it?"

I bit my lower lip, concentrating. "As a trained medium, I place my mind in a trance-like state, opening my mind to impressions. This part goes well, but as soon as I think of my father, and try to imagine what he looked like, the picture refuses to form. I draw a blank. There is nothing."

Devereaux's voice was deep and gentle. He told me a bit more about how he used hypnotism in his practice. What I could expect. How he would do it. "Considering your training in meditation, this may be far easier for you to achieve than my usual patient."

"That would be good," I said.

"That could also cause a problem. In the deep state that hypnosis produces the patient can become susceptible to suggestion. You might say things thinking only to please me or I might inadvertently suggest something which you take on as truth. I'm afraid it is not an exact science and still poorly understood."

I said nervously, "I have heard a rumor that you can tell a person in the trance to kill and they would."

He gave me a reassuring smile. "Not at all. Yours is a forceful personality and will not bend to that type of suggestion. Of course if you have it in your mind to kill someone you hate, I might convince you to commit the act, but only because that is your wish."

"Oh, I can't think of anyone I hate that much."

What Devereaux said made sense and the part of me that needed explanations felt satisfied. It helped also that his approach was like how I did a Ghost Talk for clients.

"We might not find out what is stopping you from talking with your father. I cannot predict how far we will get today, or if many sessions would get you to where you want to be."

"I understand, trust me. There are too many unknowns to predict the outcome."

He gave another one of his gentle smiles. "It's not often I get such an understanding client."

"It's not often that I'm the client instead of the practitioner," I countered. "However, I hope to be a good patient. How do we begin?"

"We begin by you looking at the spoon." His voice became lower and more sing-song. Entrancing. "Your eyes can barely stay awake. The lids are falling. You are blinking. Let the eyes close. Remember, you are safe here. You feel as if you will fall asleep at any moment. It is time to let go of everything and relax."

I was in a house. I did not recognize it. Any doors opened as I approached them and the rooms contained people I knew. Charlotte, Valentina, Jacques, Twyla, Leona, Barbier. Nowhere did I find Tristan.

Others were people I felt I couldn't quite remember. Past clients, neighbors. Some I kept in the shadows: Vonn, Parnell, Roux. I did not want to meet them.

"These are the rooms holding your memory of those you have met," said Devereaux. "I am here, and you will be safe. Nothing shall harm you. Be easy. Be calm."

Leaving one room, I entered a hall where there was a grand staircase.

"Go up the stairs, Elinor."

I went up the stairs. The walnut banister rail under my hand felt warm and smooth. Someone had applied beeswax recently, and it smelled good. There was a carpet under my feet that made me think of the one on the stairs at Hartwood. It was dark blue with accents of cream.

At the top of the stairs, I stopped. A door blocked me. Trying the handle I found it locked.

"Describe the door to me, Elinor."

It was black, with angry red letters painted across its face.

"What does it say?"

Do not enter.

"Is there anything else about the door that you see? Look closer."

Bending over, I found a tiny postscript. Squinting, I read it out loud: *By the order of Leona Granger, this door is to remain sealed.*

I'm sorry. I can't go in.

"Do you want to go in?"

Yes.

"Do you feel it is safe to go in?"

No.

"This is your mind, Elinor. You decide on what is closed to you. No one else. If you are ready to go in, I will help you. If you would rather wait another day, we shall do so."

I was never one to shirk from a challenge. My hand went to clasp the doorknob. It felt cold in my hand. Cold as ice. Before I could twist it, I saw a door open.

"The door behind you is opening, Dr. Devereaux."

"There is no door behind me, Elinor. It is your door."

"It's the door behind the painting. The secret door! Watch out!"

As she struck him from behind, the spoon flew out of his hand. Spinning and spinning, and spinning away.

Epilogue

I awoke to a smell I knew well from my visits to Charlotte's morgue. There was a hard surface under the palm of my hand. A wood floor, uneven and old. My head was splitting. Groaning, I opened my eyes.

I was no longer at Hartwood. This was some dusty old empty room stripped bare of furnishings.

Lying opposite me was Josephine Baudelaire. She was dead; her features smashed, the eyes gone. Her mouth, gaping in a silent scream, showed her tongue to be missing.

Someone had made sure that a Ghost Talker would never hear the story of how she died.

She was silenced. Forever.

Find more great reads
by Byrd Nash
at her website
ByrdNash.com

Author Notes

Dear Reader, thank you for being patient with me on this book. 2023 did not go as planned. As some of you know, we made a big move from Oklahoma to Illinois, my husband changed jobs, and we ended up doing a lot of home renovating. Thankfully, things are now calmer (or as calm as it ever gets in our household).

A big thank you to Davida, Amirah, Giselle, and Karen S., for helping on the final clean up of the book. You all constantly amaze me and I appreciate all the typo-killing you do for me.

If you love this series, can you please, take a moment and drop a review at your favorite online bookseller, Bookbub, or Goodreads? Reviews by readers is what interests other readers, and your enthusiasm also inspires me!

BYRD NASH

NOTE: This fantasy world is inspired by 1910 France, but is not a part of it.

For convenience sake, American spellings have been chosen for this fantasy series. For example, instead of grey, gray is used.

For use in this fantasy world, Guardia refers to an individual police officer. Gendarmes to the police force, or a group of police officers.

CAST OF CHARACTERS

- **Elinor Chalamet** (Shall-ah-may)— A Ghost Talker residing in the city of Alenbonné (Alan-bon-ay) in the country of Sarnesse (Sar-nessie).
- **Tristan Fontaine** Duke of Archambeau (Are-shem-bow)— is a member of Alenbonné nobility, **Le beau idéal**. For simplicity, duke is only capitalized when it is used with his title, either Duke de Archambeau or Duke de Chambaux (province title).

Tristan's circle:

- **Minette Fontaine**, the previous Duchesse de Chambaux— (deceased) wife of Tristan.
- **The Duchesse de Chambaux** (Shem-beau)— Tristan's mother.
- **Lady Valentina Fontaine**— Tristan's sister.

Elinor's circle:

- **Augustus Chalamet**— Elinor's father was murdered almost 13 years ago when Elinor was 17.
- **Dr. Charlotte LaRue** (Lah-roo)— the city's coroner and university instructor, and a friend of Elinor's.
- **Jacques Moreau** (More-row)— a childhood friend of Elinor's who is now a soldier.

The Morpheus Society:

- **Twyla Andricksson**— Elinor's former apprentice, now under the guidance of Leona Granger.
- **Leona Granger**— Elinor's mentor in The Morpheus Society.
- **Parnell Lafayette**— a member of the The Morpheus Society who wanted to achieve immortality in the Beyond (see *Spirit Guide*).
- **Lady Alouette Sarte**— (deceased) founder of the The Morpheus Society.

Law Enforcement:

- **Sven De Windt**— a senior prosecutor for the Crown. See *Gray Lady*.
- **Inspector Marcellus Barbier** (Bahr-bee-er)— a police inspector who Elinor works with to solve crimes.
- **Sergeant Quincy Dupont** (Dew-pon)— Barbier's subordinate.

Ghosts and Clients:

- **The Gold Souls** (four women, deceased)— Renee Bassett, a flute; Louisa Bonnet, a harp; Meike Roord, a cello, and Frida Korver, a violin. See *Spirit Guide*.
- **Dr. Armand Devereaux**— an alienist who heals minds. He works at Bellwether, a charity hospital, while maintaining a private practice. An acquaintance of Charlotte's.
- **Mysir Forrest Boutin**— a wool merchant who fears being buried alive.

Others:

- **Lady Josephine Baudelaire** (Bowed-lair)— a society lady who was once Minette's friend and who grew up near the Chambaux family estate. She was blackmailing Valentina over the incident of the stairs.
- **Lady Annabel van den Berg**— a young lady who was guest at Hartwood when she met an unfortunate accident arranged by Valentina and Josephine as a prank.
- **Lady Maryegold Talleyrand**— a member of the House of Lords, well-known for her diplomatic powers. She is closely related to the king.
- **Theodoor Vischeer**— a naturalist at the university. A member of the Groendykes, a lesser noble family.
- **Lady Tulip Langenberg**— goddaughter and ward of the king after the events in *Delicious Death*.
- **Lord Jansen Buckard**— A member of the nobility who attacked Lady Tulip. See *Delicious Death*.
- **Dr. Hagen**— the king's physician.
- **General Reynard Somerville**— Jacques' military superior.

Servants and Helpers:

- **Anne-Marie Draper**— Elinor's servant, a daughter of a sailor.
- **Marcus**— an orphaned street urchin who occasionally helps Elinor.
- **Stephan**— Tristan's clerk, who likes to play pranks.
- **Ruben**— a footman at the duke's townhouse, Hartwood
- **Luca**— the duke's valet.
- **Madame Darly**— the duke's cook at his townhouse, Hartwood.

- **Farrow and Styles**— bodyguards assigned to Elinor by Tristan.
- **Brigitta Meijer**— the Chalamet maid at the time of her father's murder who quit the day before.

Hotel staff:

- **Gerhard Perdersen**— the Crown hotel's head chef.
- **Henri Colbert**— the Crown's manager.
- **Pierre**— Crown head waiter.

Ghosts:

- **Four women used by Parnell Lafayatte**: Renee Bassett, Louisa Bonnet, Meike Roord, and Frida Korver. See *Spirit Guide*.

Ghost Theory & the Morpheus Society:

- **The Morpheus Society**— an intellectual group of amateurs who study the paranormal using scientific methods. Founded by Lady Alouette Sarte.
- **The 3 planes**— Physical where living humans reside; the Beyond, a transitional place where ghosts reside when not in the physical plane; and the Afterlife.
- **Ghost Talking** (not to be confused with a séance)— raises the dead to see their last memories through a ritual used by those trained by the Morpheus Society.
- **Spirit Projection**— this is a moving mind-image (Ghost Talking) that can be created from the memories of the recently dead.
- **Noise Ghost**— is a Poltergeist and uses energy from around it to cause trouble.

- **Walking Ghost**— A mysterious spirit entity with little known about it except that it is often attached to a place or family.
- **Gray Lady**— or a White Lady. Also a Walking Ghost.
- **Repeater**— a ghost attached to a specific place. Reenacts the same behavior and usually is not intelligent.
- **Possession**— A ghost inhabiting a human body and taking control of it. An uncommon occurrence and usually short term in duration due to the amount of energy a ghost needs to maintain a connection with a human.
- **Binding**— when a living person holds a soul captive, preventing the dead from transitioning to the Afterlife.
- **Attachment**— when a ghost won't let go of a person or an obsession and exists in the Beyond, refusing to transition to the Afterlife.
- **Sundering**— a process in which the soul is destroyed so it can no longer exist in any of the three plans.
- **Death Remembered**— sentimental jewelry for mourning, often holding a photo or lock of hair of the deceased.

Countries:

- **Sarnesse** (Sar-nessie)— a land of rolling hills, with an extensive coastline. Vineyards. Provinces. **King Guénard** (Gie-nar) is the ruler with an elected parliament.
- **Zulskaya** (Zul-sky-a)— the closest neighbor with a large land border. Mountainous.
- **Perino** (Pa-rin-o)— a country of tropical rain forest, separated from Sarnesse by an ocean.
- **Pendel**— a seaside resort

Addresses:

- **Madame** (Ma-dahm)— address for any financially independent and professional woman or those who are married that are not of the nobility. Any woman managing her own household. Also, A spinster would be addressed as madam.
- **Mys** (Miss)— address for financially dependent young ladies, and unmarried débutantes. Typically denotes an immaturity in the title of address.
- **Lady**— address denotes a woman of upper class, nobility.
- **Mysir** (my-sur)— address to any man, suitable for all social levels.
- **Lord**— address to any man of clear nobility, or title.

Made in the USA
Columbia, SC
18 October 2024

44669140R10120